INTO THE TAU

The light faded as Dumarest began to walk toward the Tau, leaving the enigmatic object apparently unsupported and shining with a soft effulgence.

Dumarest stared at it, concentrating, adjusting his attitude, forgetting those who had gone before aside from Iduna. And, walking, he stepped through time and space to a point years in the past when a happy, carefree child came skipping into a deserted study to discover something new and wonderful which held an immediate fascination.

And he became that child, running now, entranced, eager to discover what a doting parent had brought. To reach out with open arms. To fold them against the Tau. To hug it close and to press his face against the bright enchantment. To feel the faintest of tingles and to see the luminosity suddenly expand to engulf him, to take him elsewhere.

IDUNA'S UNIVERSE

E. C. Tubb

DAW BOOKS, INC.

DONALD A. WOLLHEIM, PUBLISHER

1633 Broadway
New York, N.Y. 10019

To JULIE

FIRST PRINTING, NOVEMBER 1979

1 2 3 4 5 6 7 8 9

DAW TRADEMARK REGISTERED
U.S. PAT. OFF. MARCA
REGISTRADA. HECHO EN U.S.A.

PRINTED IN U.S.A.

Chapter One

It was late afternoon when Dumarest reached the crest and he paused to look down the gentle slope of the valley and at the village it contained. A small, neat, tidy place with snug houses set in close proximity, the walls washed with a variety of pastel shades. The thread of a narrow river wound between banks thick with reeds and flowering shrubs, the stone bridge crossing it mottled and stained with lichens, softened with time. The square was clean, dotted with bright figures as women bustled about their business and men stood talking in the shadows cast by solidly built edifices. From somewhere a dog barked, the sound traveling with remarkable clarity through the sultry air.

"Home," said Arthen. His young voice held the anticipation of comfort. "Home."

For him and for the others who had been born in the valley but not for Dumarest. Even so the place held an attraction which he could appreciate; an atmosphere of gentleness and calm which if nothing else served to provide a haven from the bustle of cities, the empty coldness of space. A place in which to rest and wait and to earn what he could. One in which to hide and, perhaps, to learn.

"Earl?" Arthen was impatient to get moving. "We want to get home before dark."

"We have plenty of time."

"But—"

"And Michelle will be waiting. An hour more after so many days—what does it matter?"

Arthen blushed but made no comment, busying himself with the horses, checking their loads. Both animals carried camping gear and the fruits of the hunt; skins, teeth, the snarling mask of a feral beast which even in death radiated a chilling ferocity. Touching it he felt a warm glow. Dumarest had killed it but he had helped and so would share in the achievement. Michelle would be impressed and he had the gift of a soft pelt to further win her regard. Tonight, with luck, he would make her his own.

And Dumarest?

Arthen looked at the man now standing tall and silent on the summit of the crest. To have worked with him was an experience he would never forget. Against him other hunters were clumsy fools frightening away more game than they ever caught, lacking the calm precision, the sure knowledge which Dumarest had displayed. But he wasn't being fair and knew it. Killing was against the tenets of those who lived in the valley and only ruthless predators were hunted so as to save the domesticated stock. He looked at them grazing in the valley, herds of kine now safe against the beast which had harassed them as Dumarest was the richer by the price set on its head.

Was he thinking of that money and what it could bring?

Together with the other skins and furs it would be enough for him to leave the village and buy passage on a vessel bound for another world. Mtombo, the itinerent Hausai, would buy them from him and offer a fair price. Would he go? Or would he stay until the end of the season? If so he might be persuaded to stand at his side when Michelle was led toward him bound with the marriage ties. Arthen lost himself in speculation as he thought about it; the fires, the music, the wine and conviviality, the feast and the dancing, the good-natured horseplay attendant at every wedding. It would be good to have Dumarest at his side at such a time.

"Earl—" Impulsively he began to make the request, breaking off as Dumarest lifted a hand. "Something? You see something?"

"There are no women in the western fields. Should there be?"

Arthen frowned, thinking, then shook his head.

"Not necessarily. Those fields are set with reeds, and harvesting won't be for another month yet. Sometimes a few girls go out to gather herbs but a birth could be due and they would be assembling to greet the new life."

Dumarest nodded, he had met the custom before, one which fell into neglect as the settlements grew. "And the river? No boats?"

"The sun is lowering and the fish won't bite when the light is too bright on the water." Arthen added. "You think there could be something the matter, Earl?"

"No. I was just curious."

Curious and more than curious, checking the terrain before moving from the shelter of the trees hugging the crest, an automatic display of caution which the young man found strange. What possible danger could lie in the village?

What enemies did Dumarest have to fear?

Questions which remained unasked as they moved down the slope toward the cluster of houses. Questions which were forgotten as, with a flurry of gaily colored skirts, Michelle came running toward him.

"Arthen!"

"Michelle!"

He felt the soft, warm impact of her, the rounded mounds beneath her blouse creating a sudden heat with their feminine stimulus, one accentuated by the pressure of her thighs.

"Darling!" Her mouth was close to his, her lips moist, her breath scented with mint and roses. "It's been so long! I've missed you so much! Did you—"

"Later." He glanced to where Dumarest walked with the beasts lower down the path. "Later, Michelle, now I've work to do."

"Arthen!"

"Work," he said firmly. "The animals must be taken care of and the loads seen to and other things settled. Earl can't do it alone." A lie but one which enhanced his importance. "Is Tetray in the Communal House?"

"Probably. Mtombo flew in yesterday."

"The Hausi? I didn't see his raft."

"It dropped and will return when he sends for it. A matter of deliveries to other settlements, I think." She shrugged, dismissing uninteresting details. "Did you get it?"

"The beast?" His smile was her answer.

"Arthen!" Again he felt the warm, exciting impact of her body added to, this time, the pressure of her lips. "You're wonderful! I told them you'd do it! I told them!"

"I had help." He glanced after Dumarest and forced himself to push her away. "Later, Michelle, after things have been settled. There's something I want to ask you."

"What?" But it would be no surprise, he could tell from the expression in her eyes. "And when?"

"After we've seen Mtombo."

The agent was tall, strongly built, his face livid with caste scars which shone like beacons against the ebon skin. A trader, go-between, agent for a dozen enterprises, a man of reputation who never lied but did not always tell all of the truth. Now, his eyes enigmatic, he accepted the glass of wine handed to him by the Elder.

"Your health, Tetray!" The lift of his glass was a toast and acknowledgment of the status of his host. "And yours, Earl. A fine selection of skins and furs. We can do business, I hope?"

"We can talk, certainly."

"A cautious man." The Hausi smiled. "One who is reluctant to commit himself. Do you intend a further hunt?"

"Killing for the sake of it?" Tetray frowned and set down his glass. "I think not. To encourage the young to regard living forms as a source of revenue is against our beliefs. It is obscene to slay for the sake of skins and bone and fur."

A statement, not an opinion, and Dumarest knew better than to argue against a point of view which he shared. The Hausi, for reasons of his own, pressed the matter.

"You put it badly I think, my friend. Herds are bred and maintained for later harvesting on any of countless worlds. Kine raised for beef and leather as well as for milk. Sheep for wool and also for meat. A crop the same as wheat or corn."

"No!" Tetray shook his head. "Not the same. A beast is a life form basically similar to ourselves. It has feelings, the need to survive, the desire to breed. It suffers and can know contentment. To hunt it down, to kill it for the fur it bears— horrible!"

"Yet you engaged Earl to rid you of a pest."

"Because it was that—a pest. We lost a score of kine to it and double that number of sheep were killed and savaged. Even human life was at risk and the welfare of a child must outweigh all other considerations. There can be no expediency when dealing with the problems confronting the young." Tetray sipped at his wine and added, "We were fortunate in having an experienced man staying as a guest in our village who was willing to help us."

"But you have your own hunters," said Mtombo softly. "What of them?"

"I deplore them." Tetray looked at his wine then lifted his head to stare at the agent. "But we cannot rely on having an experienced hunter visit us when we need such an expert. We must have men trained and ready against predators from the hills."

"And those from the cities? From other worlds?"

"Men?" Tetray looked baffled. "What have we to fear from them?"

A question the Hausi didn't answer, looking instead at Dumarest who sat with his untouched wine, his eyes holding a cynical gleam.

Dumarest said, "I've mentioned it before, Tetray. You lack any protection."

"Against what?"

"Those who could do you harm. The most savage predators you could ever know come in the form of men."

"Slavers?" The Elder shrugged. "Oh, I've heard of such, but how are they to be taken seriously? And what would they want here? Onorldi is a peaceful world with no mines or installations needing a continual influx of cheap labor."

"There are ships," said Mtombo bluntly. "And it could pay to transport victims if they are easy to obtain. I mention this, my friend, because I wish you well. But as a guest I will not intrude on the subject again. But you, Earl, about your catch. Two hundred either in cash or to your credit. A deal?"

"If you include transportation to the city, yes."

"A deal." The Hausi smiled his pleasure at a successful trade. "And if you want me to arrange a passage for you I will be honored." He added dryly, "And naturally you can rely on my discretion."

A hint? A Hausi knew more than he divulged and he could have been curious as to why a man should choose to isolate himself in a secluded village. A curiosity stimulated, perhaps, by questions as to his knowledge of such a man.

Dumarest said, "I'll arrange my own passage. When do we leave?"

"My raft will return tomorrow evening. Once loaded there will be no reason for delay." Mtombo lifted his glass, a toast to seal the agreement. "We shall be in the city the following night."

And after that into space again, to travel the void to another world, to ask more questions and to continue the search. To take the clues he had and to turn them into definite answers. To find the exact location of Earth.

Outside Dumarest halted to tilt his head and stare up at the sky. It was brilliant with stars, swaths of shimmering luminescence, curtains of jewel-crusted splendor, even the dust clouds mottling the firmament edged with a sheen of scintillant glory. Too much brightness and too many stars; the view he longed to see would be relatively dark with minute dots gleaming in isolated splendor, stars set in patterns which would be signposts in the sky, the visible symbols of reassurance that he was, finally, home.

Home!

He felt the old, familiar ache, the emptiness and drag of hope too often frustrated, too often betrayed. A man alone with his heart and mind and body set on a single determination: to find the world of his birth and return to it. But Onorldi was not near to Earth. No star in this sector could be the one which warmed the planet he sought. To find it he had to move on and, already, he could have left it too late.

"Earl?" The voice whispered from the shadows. "Is that you, Earl?"

"Who is it?" He relaxed as a figure stepped into view, starlight silvering the hair, deepening the lines graven on sunken cheeks. "Hainan, what can I do for you?"

"For me nothing, Earl, but Lenz is opening a new vat to celebrate young Arthen getting up the courage to ask for Michelle's hand in marriage and, naturally, you have to join us." He stepped a little closer and Dumarest could tell from his breath the man hadn't waited for company to begin his celebrations. "It's good wine, Earl."

Thick and rich and served in goblets carved from a finely grained wood the natural scent of the timber adding an extra dimension to the pungency of the wine. Dumarest sipped and nodded his appreciation.

"You like it, Earl?" Lenz beamed as he lifted a jug and refilled drained goblets. "Three years in the making and I'm not going to tell you what went into it. Something special I've saved to celebrate my daughter's betrothal." He added, grinning, "And I've something even better put by for the first birthing."

"The first and many to follow," said Hainan holding out his empty container. "Your health, Lenz."

"Your health!"

The toast roared to shake the air of the cellar in which they were gathered. A blast which shook the flames riding on the squat bodies of candles, causing them to dance and, in the guttering light, the faces of those invited seemed to shift and move and to adopt strange and eerie configurations. A moment only and then the illusion was past and they seemed what they were; a group of friends gathered to drink and share the happiness of their host.

"Arthen's a good lad," said Lenz. "And I know Michelle's been waiting for him to speak for a long time now. In fact I was just getting ready to have a quiet word with the boy myself." He smiled at his clenched hand—he would never have used it and they all knew it. "But thanks to Earl that wasn't necessary."

"Why?" said a man. "What did he do?"

"Took him out, kept him away, made him hungry for a little comfort. There's nothing like a good, long hunt to get the juice rising in a man. Right, lad?"

Arthen grunted. He sat in the rear with his back against a wall one shoulder leaning against a barrel and had remained invisible until now. From his expression Dumarest guessed that he would have preferred to remain that way.

He said, "Arthen didn't need encouraging. In fact he damned near ran my legs off. Now I know why he was in such a hurry to get back."

The man who had spoken before said dryly, "Maybe he was afraid of getting hurt."

"No."

"No?" The man reached out and rested his fingers on Dumarest's tunic. The plastic was scarred, glints of metal showing from the buried mesh. "A close thing, eh?"

"Shut up, Marl," said Lenz sharply.

"I was only asking. Those rips look to me as if caused by claws. Maybe someone wasn't doing his job?"

Someone too tense who had acted too slowly. The beast had been killed but there had been a mate and Arthen who should have maintained watch had been taken by surprise.

Things Dumarest didn't mention and the boy was glad of it but he was too honest to remain silent.

"I slipped," he admitted. "There was a mate and I fired too late and missed. The second shot only wounded it and it took three days to track it down."

Lenz said sharply, "But it's dead?"

"Yes. A gravid female. Earl got it with a long shot and knocked it from a ridge. It fell into a crevasse and it would have been too difficult to have recovered the body."

"But it's dead?"

"It's dead. Earl made sure of that."

Lenz sighed his relief. "Thank God for that. A gravid female—a few months and we'd have been overrun with the things."

"And would have been if it had been left to Arthen." Marl tore at the incident like a dog worrying a bone. A man betraying his jealousy and frustration and doing his best to rob his successful rival of his moment of triumph. "It was a mistake to have sent him out. No boy can hope to do a man's job."

"But a boy can learn," said Dumarest. "And when he does he stops being a boy." More loudly he said, "Arthen, tomorrow you pick up a half of the bounty due on the beast. I've arranged it with Tetray."

"A half?"

"Your share. You earned it."

And would enjoy what the money could bring. A good wedding with gifts for all and a reputation which would last until he grew old. The simple way of villages locked as they were in their own small enclaves. Standing in the cellar, sipping his wine, watching the undisguised merriment of those assembled, Dumarest could envy their uncomplicated existence. To grow, to marry, to breed, to age and finally to die. Life matched in harmony with the seasons with always the comfort of friends at hand and even the small differences and bickerings lost in the general sweep of the years. There would be pain, true, for no life could be free of that as no life could be free of anguish and grief and disappointments and frustrations, but all would be on a relatively minor scale. And the curse of more complex societies, the screaming loneliness which walked like a plague through congested cities, that at least would be absent.

"Earl?" Lenz was at his side, jug lifted. "More wine?"

"A little."

"Let me fill it to the brim." The man acted even as he spoke. "Of all here you deserve it most."

"Appreciate it, maybe."

"That too and I wish I could give you a cargo of it but I was thinking of the boy. Marl—well he can't hold his drink and says more than he should. Tomorrow he'll regret it and apologize." Pausing, Lenz added, "I hear you'll be leaving us tomorrow."

"Yes."

"A pity. You fit in well and you'll be missed. If you should change your mind or want to return you're welcome to stay as my guest for as long as you want."

"Thank you," said Dumarest. "I'll remember that."

"Just don't forget it." Lenz stared at the jug in his hand, blinked then thrust it forward. "Take it," he urged. "There could be someone you'd like to share a farewell drink with. A woman, perhaps." He swayed, more affected by the wine than he realized, his words beginning to slur. "There're quite a few who'd like to take you to bed if you were to tap on their windows. Marry you too if you've a mind to settle down. A man needs to get himself married. I—" He broke off and rubbed at his face. "Odd. I feel funny. I guess I need some air."

They all needed air. That in the cellar had grown foul, the flames of the candles burning low as they fought to dispel the gloom. Taking the jug, Dumarest headed for the stairs.

"I'll leave the door open," he said. "Have a good time."

The door was thick, well-fitting, forming an airtight seal. It yielded to his weight and Dumarest passed through into the house. He paused, sniffing, seeing lights move beyond the windows flanking the heavy door leading to the street. Heading toward it he kicked something soft and, stooping, found a middle-aged woman lying unconscious on the floor. Lenz's wife lying with her mouth open and breathing in a stertorous rasp. Dumarest sniffed at her lips then rose and moved softly toward the windows.

Looking outside, his face took on the pitiless ferocity of the beast he had hunted and killed.

The lights were close, portable beams held by individuals, a floodlight throwing brilliance from a low-drifting raft holding

supervising figures. As he watched, a door was burned open
and shapes moved to search inside the house. A moment and
they reappeared bearing limp figures which they heaved into
the raft. Items of choice selected by those who knew their
trade.

Slavers at work.

They had come under cover of darkness, traveling low so
as to avoid detection against the sky. Once they had reached
the village, gas had done its work; invisible, insidious vapor
which had covered the area to stun and eliminate all
resistance. A compound quick to act and quick to disperse—
only those in the cellar could have escaped its affect.

Only the handful of near-drunken men could offer any
form of resistance.

It wasn't enough.

Dumarest thought about it as he watched from the dark-
ened room, assessing chances even as he recognized limita-
tions. They needed guns but aside from those used in the
hunt and now safely locked away none were to be found in
the village. A peace-loving community had no use for tools
designed to kill. But there were other things; pitchforks, flails,
scythes—yet even the crudest weapon needed a determined
man behind it if it was to be any use. Arthen would fight for
Michelle but to fight was not enough. He had to win. And
would Marl fight? Hainan? Could they if they wanted? Did
they know how?

And, even if they did, how effective would they be in their
present condition?

Time! If he could only gain time!

Those gassed would recover and when they did the odds
would be against the slavers. Delay them long enough and
the operation would have to be abandoned. Kill enough of
the slavers and the rest would withdraw—there was no profit
in getting killed. But one man against so many?

"Lena?" The voice was a petulant whisper. "Where are
you, woman? Why is the house so dark?" Lenz rising like a
ghost from the cellar, confused, unaware of the passage of
time. He swore as he stumbled and fell. "Lena?"

He reared as Dumarest grabbed him, fighting against the
hand clamped over his mouth, relaxing as he recognized the
voice at his ear.

"Listen," said Dumarest softly. "Don't move, just listen."

He explained the situation, felt the man he was holding convulse with incredulous shock, and eased his grip only when certain there would be no noisy arguments or protestations.

Lenz, abruptly cold sober, said, "What can we do, Earl?"

"That's up to you. You've a choice but I'm not going to make it for you. You can hide, yield or fight."

"Give up? Never!"

"Then stay in the cellar and pray you aren't found or get out and do what damage you can." Dumarest glanced at the window as the sound of breaking wood came from lower down the street. "They're moving closer. You'd better make up your mind."

"If we hit their rafts would that do it?"

"It could."

"The guards?"

"Hit them too if you can."

"And you, Earl?" Then, as Dumarest remained silent, Lenz added, "I've no right to ask that you help us and I know it, but I wish you would. We could use someone who knows what to do. Advice, even—can't you give us that?"

"You don't need advice," said Dumarest. "You need guts. Just think of what is going to happen to Michelle if those slavers make off with her. Your daughter and the others like her. Your young men and wives if they're strong and healthy enough. You know what it's like in a mine? In an undersea installation? Set to till fields in the middle of nowhere with a pint of water a day as the only ration in a temperature hot enough to cook eggs? Slaves are cheap. Living machines to be used and thrown aside when old or ill. On some worlds they go to feed animals when their time is done. Think of it, Lenz. You work like a dog all your life then get thrown to a beast as a reward."

"I'd die first!"

"Maybe."

"I mean it, Earl!"

"So you mean it. So mean it now. Die if you have to but take a few of those bastards with you. Get close and use a knife if there's no other way. Aim for the guts and rip upward. What the hell can you lose?"

A crash sounded close before the man could answer. Dumarest stepped to the window, looked at the lights, the shapes outside, returned to join Lenz.

"They're close," he whispered. "Decide what you're going to do and get on with it. If you choose to hide, fasten the cellar door in some way. If to run, get moving right away. Get those men up and out of here. Leave by the rear, keep apart, keep silent. Even if they see you they may not bother to run you down but they won't spot you if you're careful. As far as they're concerned everyone is unconscious and waiting collection."

"Run," said Lenz. "Who said anything about running? I mean to fight."

"Maybe."

"To fight, Earl." Lenz looked at Dumarest, his eyes gleaming with reflected light as a beam hit the window to be diffused and sent glowing about the room. "Even if I fight alone. It's my daughter, remember."

"I haven't forgotten. Make sure Arthen doesn't. Hurry now—move!"

Dumarest watched as scrambles came from the cellar, mutters, a stifled curse and once the meaty impact of a fist. Lenz was learning. Peace was a good thing when applied to animals but suicidal when used to tame men who had the heritage of monsters. Force recognized only one effective argument—greater force.

And all Dumarest had was his knife.

He eased in where it rode in his boot, nine inches of honed and polished steel, needle-pointed and razor-edged, the hilt worn to his hand. With it he could cut and slash and stab, but used in that way the weapon was only effective to the reach of his arm. Thrown, it was lost and, even if it hit was a one-time thing only.

His knife and his brain and the speed of his body. Things which had served him before and now must do so again. Basics which, together with luck, were the instruments he must use in order to survive.

But luck was a wanton jade and a fickle mistress—how could he be sure it still rode with him?

"Earl!" Lenz whispered from where he stood with the others at the rear of the house. "There's a slaver out here. Armed and watching. What shall we do?"

Run, make the break, accept your dead and fight on. The simple mercenary creed which valued life for what it was, a saleable and disposable commodity. But Lenz was not and had never been a mercenary and neither had the others. Life, to them, was too precious and too weakening. Love of life made them cowards.

"Watch," said Dumarest. "When the guard moves, make your break. And fight, damn you! Fight!"

He reached for the door as the lights shifted and the raft veered. The moment he had waited for and the one giving the best chance. He was outside and running before they spotted him; then the standing figure on the raft called out with imperious command, "That man! Get him!"

A woman, the pitch and tone were unmistakable, and even as Dumarest threw himself down to roll as dirt plumed from the street he could see her grotesquely painted face.

"Don't kill him, you fools! Get him!"

Splinters of light shone from gilded nails and teeth, the lips were set with ridged gems, the lids of the eyes held tattooed patterns, the lobes of the ears supported massed crystal. The armor matched the bizarre ensemble; ridges and points and curves set in eye-wrenching array all tinted and glowing with enamelled fire.

And as she so her followers; women all, dressed in the fabric of nightmare, enjoying their trade, spicing it with bursts of wanton cruelty as the ruby smears on their whips and hands testified.

Sadists.

Maniacs.

Creatures living in a world created by drugs and the tortuous sinuosities of diseased brains. The night had shielded them and slanted his judgment. A normal slaver would accept ransom; from these degenerates he could hope for nothing.

Rising, he looked around. Behind him figures waited armed, ready and eager to blast his legs into masses of pulped flesh and shattered bone. To either side stood others and before him, beyond the raft, yet more. The woman riding the vehicle was accompanied by two others each now holding a laser.

"As you can see, it is useless to resist," she said. "Now tell me how it is that you are conscious when you should be comatose. How did you avoid the effects of the gas?"

"I have an antidote, my lady."

"And you used it?"

"Of course."

"Which means that you knew we were coming. That, alone, shows you for the liar you are. None could have known of our plans. The truth now, quickly!"

"I have been a slaver myself and always carry the antidote. I couldn't sleep and saw you arrive. I recognized the taint of the gas and, well, the rest should be obvious. For ransom I offer—"

"I am not interested in your ransom."

"—the information as to where you can find a settlement of two thousand men and women all in prime condition," he continued blandly. "Or if you would prefer cash I have credit with a Hausi. His name is Mtombo—you may already have found him."

"His skin will make good leather for my gloves." The whip flicked in her hand. "Come closer, man. Halt! That is close enough. You interest me. Few men bother to lie so convincingly when faced with danger. It means that you have a cool brain of a trusting faith in what gods you choose to worship. Valladia?"

"Kill him," said the woman to her right. "Let me do it. I will fry his genitals and watch as he screams."

"Hylda?"

"Alive he is worth money."

"True, and you, my sweet, love money like others love life. As much as Valladia loves the spectacle of pain. Well, maybe you can both be satisfied. Now we have work to do. Ristine! Take care of our prize!"

She came from behind, a pad in one hand, the scent of anesthetics rising from the fabric. A clumsy means to render him unconscious, a hypogun would have fired its charge through skin and fat and into the bloodstream at the pressure of a finger. A mistake, one to add to those already made, the flanking guards facing each other, mutual targets should they open fire. Those at the rear who would cut down those behind the raft. The risk always taken by any who tried to surround a quarry and who failed to realize that the mere display of force could contain the seeds of its own destruction.

"Ristine," said Dumarest. "A nice name. One I have heard before."

"Shut your mouth!"

"Was it in a palace?" he mused as she came closer. "In the theater? No, I remember now. It was in a brothel. She earned a living by polishing the floor."

A weak insult and a stupid one in normal times but it served to inflame her anger and make her that little more careless. She reached him, left arm sliding over his left shoulder to hold him close, the pad sweeping around in her right hand to press over his face.

And, for that moment, she was shielding his rear from those behind.

Dumarest lifted his right hand, caught her wrist, twisted, released the broken limb as his left hand trapped her other arm. Three steps forward and he felt her jerk as a laser burned a hole into her kidneys; then he had stooped, using the power of back and shoulders to hurl her over his head and toward the facing guards, a target at which they instinctively fired as he dived to hit the ground, to roll, to slash out with his blade and feel the edge bite and drag through flesh and sinew as it hamstrung a guard and fetched her down, screaming, as above them both fire and flame sent death to whine and burn through the fire.

A moment in which he turned, arm lifting, steel flashing as it hurtled through the air to find the throat of the woman who had wanted to smile as he screamed in pain. As Valladia fell, coughing a thick, red stream, he snatched up the fallen guard's rifle and fired. Again. Again.

And cursed as the weapon jammed.

"Cease firing!" Hylda shouted the command from where she stood, now alone, on the raft. "You fools! Cease firing! Barbra! Anna! Take him!"

One went down as Dumarest swung the useless rifle, the stock splintering in a ruin to match her skull, crushed beneath the ornate helmet. The other shrieked as he darted in, weaving, stabbing with the splintered remains and bringing blood spurting from jagged punctures. A third, appearing from shadows, fell back doubled and vomiting from a kick in the stomach. Then again came the sound of firing, the vicious snarl of bullets and a blow which slammed against the side of his head to send him down to the dirt. Dazed, he twisted, rolling to rise on hands and knees, to stare at the widening pool of blood which reflected the stars, blurring outlines of his own, tormented face.

Chapter Two

The day had started badly and promised to get worse. At dawn a man had been impaled before the palace and his screams and moans would last for days as, slowly, he died. A barbaric form of execution and one she would like to abolish; but old customs died hard and none had mercy on those guilty of rape. Three cases of hnaudifida had been reported from the northeastern sector, and unless the restrictions she had imposed were effective the disease could spread with consequent loss of valuable slaves. And now it looked like rain.

From the window of her room she could see the clouds gathering over the distant mountains. Masses of seething gray, harsh and ugly against the pale emerald of the sky, the sun itself now shielded behind strands of waterlogged vapor. If the wind held there could be trouble. With the rain would come thunder and lightning, hail, floods of water which would flatten crops now almost ready for harvesting. She must see if rafts could be sent to seed the clouds and vent their contents safely in the foothills. Or perhaps Tamiras, with his electronic barriers, could be of help. His demonstration had been impressive, but a working installation couldn't be guaranteed to work and the cost was enormous.

And yet possibly worth it. On Esslin storms could bring ruin in more ways than one.

"My lady?" Shamarre, as silent as always, had approached as she stood engrossed at the window. Now she stood, as stolid as granite, thickly muscled arms disguised by her blouse, the trunks of thighs and the corded sinews of stomach and torso taut against the covering fabric. An Amazon dedicated to her service. "Is something bothering you?"

The question was a liberty taken with the confidence of long familiarity. Who else would have dared to speak to The ruler of Esslin in such a manner? For a moment Kathryn mused over the problem then, impatiently, dismissed it. What did it matter?

"My lady, you—"

"I know." Kathryn turned from the window. The guard-attendant would mention her appointments, urge haste, give unwanted advice and in general make herself a nuisance but, when the woman again spoke, she realized she had been mistaken.

"You have time to relax a little," said Shamarre doggedly. "A bath, even. Certainly something to take the stink of execution from your nostrils."

"You disapprove?"

"The man had to die. You didn't have to attend."

A mistake and one she knew all too well. Even though she was Matriarch yet still she was the prisoner of custom and Shamarre must know it. To have absented herself would have been to give tacit disapproval of the execution, and the injured woman would have felt herself affronted. She had friends and they would have taken her side. A schism would have been created, one which could have come to nothing or which could have resulted in a vicious outbreak of destructive hostility.

It had happened before. Too often it had happened before.

There was no time to indulge in the long, lingering luxury of a bath and to take a dip would be to ruin her cosmetics and waste more time than would be saved. But Tamiras had recently installed one of his electro-baths and it was good to relax on the padded cushions and feel the impulse of invisible energies as they massaged skin and muscle with random, stimulating contractions and expansions of balanced fields.

Lying in a cat-like dose, not asleep and yet not fully awake, she thought of the inventor and his claims. A pity he was a man; she could appreciate the difficulties beneath which he labored trying to convince those who had money and influence that he was not a misguided dreamer. This bath was proof that he was far from that and an extension of the idea could replace the need for water in arid areas. Electro-currents could remove dirt and scale and dead epidermis and leave the body clean without a drop of water being needed. Properly handled and promoted, the invention could earn a fortune.

Would he leave Esslin if it did?

She hoped not. There was something likeable about the man despite his wizened appearance and abruptly aggressive mannerisms. True, he was sly in his slanted insults and innuendoes, but much could be forgiven a man of demonstrated talent. She must talk to him, take advice on the matter, ask Gustav for his opinion. That, at least, should please him—not often did she consult with her consort.

Closing her eyes, she looked at the face of her husband painted from memory against the inner surface of the lids.

Young—they had both been young. Strong enough in his fashion and handsome as any with hair piled high in a crested mane and eyes which, in their subtle slant, seemed to hold an inner wisdom. Eyes which contained a secret laughter which had made light of her early worries. The mirth which he had used as armor against the slights and hurts time and the pressure of office had brought. He was a man chosen to impregnate her womb and there had been too many to remind him of that. Too many to drive home his basic insignificance. A stallion selected for his lineage to father the future rulers of Esslin. To sire the daughters which—

No!

No—it was better she did not think of that.

Of the first miscarriage following the news of the rebellion when Clarice Duvhal had turned the entire southern region into flame with the aid of hired mercenaries. Of the second when she had been almost assassinated by a rival—the unborn child giving its life to save her own. Of the successful birth when, finally, she had lifted her daughter in her arms and felt the glow of true happiness.

One that had failed to last.

"My lady?" Shamarre was standing at her side. "You feel rested?"

"Yes." A touch and the humming, easing contact of the fields ceased. "Fetch me wine."

Drinking it, she stared into a mirror and studied the familiar lines and contours of her face. One which had worn too long now to ever hope that it could turn into a thing of beauty. It held strength and determination, she knew—without either of those attributes she would never have been able to survive—but the brows were too thick and straight, the lips too thin, the jaw too prominent, the nose too hooked.

Gustav had made fun of it.

"You are a strong and lovely bird, my dear. One who sits and watches and strikes when the need arises. Other women are cats or mice or foxes. Many are spiders. You, above all, are honest."

How little had he known!

Or had he really known but had played the game in the only way it could be played if either was to find a degree of contentment in their union? And, certainly, when he had come to her after the birth and stooped to kiss her she had seen that within his eyes which had given her food for thought. An expression repeated when he had, later, kissed the child. A tenderness. A yearning. A look which could have been one of love.

"My lady!"

"Yes, I know. Time is passing and duty calls." She finished the wine and threw the woman the empty glass. "Well, what is next on the agenda?"

"Maureen Clairmont of the Elguard Marsh needs more workers if she is to expand her holdings as she intends. If she is allowed to bid unchecked, the price will rise to the detriment of others."

And, should she grow too strong, would be a source of potential trouble.

"I'll see to it. And?"

"A meeting with the Hsi-Wok Combine."

Entrepreneurs who, like hungry dogs, were eager for the chance to tear at a bone. Give them their way and within a decade they would have gutted the planet and turned it into a cesspool of vice.

"And?"

A list of trivia which she could have done without and would ignore should the need arise. But such work served to fill the hours and, while thinking of the minutiae of rule, she could lessen the impact of despair. One item caused her to frown.

"Hylda Vroom? On the field?"

"Yes, my lady."

"Didn't she join up with some slavers?"

"Yes, my lady. With Abra Merenda. Apparently she got herself killed during their last raid and Hylda took over the command."

And brought her catch to where she knew there was a

market. Kathryn nodded, thinking the incident might be put to good advantage. An open auction with primed bidders who would force up prices against Maureen Clairmont and so make it uneconomical for her to expand. With luck she could be left with ridiculously expensive slaves and the display of bad judgment on her part would turn any backers she might have against her.

The plan amused her. It was better than a naked display of open force which, while demonstrating that it was she who ruled and none other, could arouse dissension. To make the woman look a fool would be sweet revenge.

Then she lost her smile as the communicator hummed. Answering it, Shamarre turned, her face a mask.

"The monk," she said. "He is waiting, my lady. In the Octagonal Room."

He stood in the exact center as if taking up the position to maintain the symmetry of the chamber. Eight walls, each elaborately carved with depictions of men and animals locked in attitudes of combat or mutual caresses; the skill of the artist made it impossible to be certain. Tints and colors interwoven to give the impression of garments, of fur and feather and scale, of gossamer and hair and glitters which could have been the exudations of natural fluids. Lights were carefully positioned to accentuate suggestive shadows and, together, the panels formed a series designed to catch and hold the attention, to intrigue, to shock, to startle.

The roof matched the walls, groined, fluted, carved and colored to give the appearance of the interior of a shell. The floor was a polished mosaic which traced a complex pattern. There were no furnishings. Had he wanted to sit, the monk would have had to squat on the floor, but Brother Remick had no desire to sit. He was accustomed to waiting.

He was tall, old, the thrown-back cowl of his brown, homespun robe framing a near-bald skull, a face lined with privation and relieved only by the burning intelligence and compassion of his deep-set eyes, the lips which curved in gentle humor. Rough sandals hugged his naked feet and the hands which he held folded before him displayed swollen knuckles and wrists.

A dedicated man who had chosen to serve the Universal Church which preached that all men were brothers and the pain of one was the anguish of all. And that if all could but recognize the truth of the credo, *there, but for the love of God, go I*, the millennium would have arrived.

He would never live to see it. No monk now alive would see it but, one day, it would come and until it did he would do what he could to ease the lives of those who needed help.

Now he could only wait until Kathryn Acchabaron, Matriarch of Esslin, should condescend to hear his report.

She came sooner than he expected and one look at his face was enough.

"You failed!" From the first she had known it and yet hope had survived. Now the old, familiar sickness and despair turned into a sudden and vicious rage. "You failed! I should have you stripped and beaten and impaled! You fool! You useless fool!"

"Sister—"

"Don't call me that! I'm not one of your spineless flock! I am the ruler of this world and you had best not forget it!"

Pride blazed from her as if she had been a fire and with it came the arrogance of wealth, the indifference to the concern of others which he had met so often before. He dealt with it now as he had then, standing, waiting for the emotional storm to pass, ready to submit without argument to any punishment she might choose to inflict. The way of those serving the Church which had gained scars and dealt for many of them, respect for many more. Always the strong can recognize an equal strength even if demonstrated in a manner different from their own.

Now, calming, she said, "What happened? Report!"

"As you say, my lady, I did not succeed. I found it beyond my skill to aid the poor creature you placed in my care. But how could it be otherwise?"

"You are a master of hypnotism and skilled in medical science." As he lifted his head she made an impatient gesture. "Don't bother to deny it. I've had you watched and know of your work among the poor. The medications you give them, the operations you perform, the manner in which you eradicate pain."

"Herbs," he said gently. "The lancing of boils and the setting of broken limbs. A little suggestion—there is nothing harmful in that, my lady."

"Did I say there was? Am I even blaming you? I'd

hoped—God, how I'd hoped—but never mind." She drew in her breath, accepting what she could not avoid, another failure to add to the rest. "Your work is done here. You may go."

Brother Remick said, "Before I do, my lady. May I have a word?'

"Well?"

"You asked too much of my poor skill. How could I hope to succeed where others have failed. And there have been others? Men trained in the field of mental sickness?"

Men and women both and all demanding high rewards for accomplishing nothing. As she had expected the monk to make a demand. As he still might make it.

"Yes," she admitted. "So?"

"Let others make the attempt. We have those in the Church more skilled than myself. If you could arrange passage I am confident that some progress could be made."

"Passage? To where?"

To Hope, she assumed, where the Church had their headquarters or to Pace where they had their great medical establishment. She blinked at the answer.

"To Elysium, my lady. A world not too distant from Esslin."

"And the cost?"

Again he surprised her. "The cost of the journey naturally, but once on Elysium there will be no charge. You will merely donate what you wish to give." He added quietly, "If you were sick, dying of a malignancy which could be cured, would you appreciate your life being set in the scales against what you owned? Or if one dear to you were ill would you thank those who refused to cure her because you could not afford to meet their fees?"

"Charity?" Her laugh was strained. "You believe in charity?"

"We believe in doing to others as we would like them to do to us. You may have heard that before, my lady. It is known as the Golden Rule."

Was he rebuking her? For a moment she suspected it then recognized the ridiculousness of the suspicion. On this world no man, not even a monk, could have been such a fool.

"My lady, you summoned me and I came and did what I could, for we of the Church never refuse any in need. Now you have given me leave to go. Before I do may I crave a boon?"

The reward he wanted—what would it be? Cynicism sharpened her tones.

"You disappoint me, monk. For once I had hoped to have found a man who practiced what he preached. One willing to give without demanding a return. Well, what do you want? Money?"

"Permission, my lady." Startled, she heard him press on. "Your permission to set up the Church at the edge of the field. Twice we have tried and each time the guards have thrown it down. Brother Juba was injured the last time and Brother Echo is tending him at this moment. Both are old."

"And?" She waited for him to continue. Some comforts for his companions, surely. If he called them old they must be almost doddering. What brought men like that to share such poverty? "Speak, man," she demanded. "What else?"

"Nothing, my lady."

"Nothing?" She gave a curt laugh. "Just my permission to set up your church? You have it. A hundred square yards— not closer than the same distance from the gate."

The reward of failure. How would Gustav take it? She must go to him at once.

He was within his study, seated at his desk, busy with a litter of papers, old books, mouldering tomes from a host of worlds brought by traders who knew of his interest. For a moment she stood watching him from the open door then, as if sensing her presence, he turned and rose to face her.

"Kathryn!"

He gave his usual, impeccable bow, a gesture which was as much a part of him as the trick he had of touching his left eyebrow when mastering his anger. A thing she had not seen since the fool from Elkan had given his verdict and made his suggestion. She wondered if his back still bore the scars she had ordered to be placed there.

"Gustav!" She lifted her hands as he advanced and smiled as he took them and lifted them to his lips. A smile which vanished as he looked at her. "No, my dear. Again—no!"

She felt him near her, his arms around her, all protocol forgotten in this moment of her need. A weakness, no Matriarch could ever lean on another, but it was good to know that she was not alone, that there was another to share her

grief, her empty yearning. And he had the right. Of all men
he had the right.

"Don't give up hope," he whispered. "We can try again.
There will be someone with courage enough or skill enough.
Dear God, there has to be someone!"

He turned as his voice broke, unwilling to let her see the
tears in his eyes, the haggard expression he knew must be
marring his face. Did she recognize his contempt? Share it?
Know him for the coward he was? And yet was sheer
willingness enough? Arnold had been young and strong and
willing and where was Arnold now? Charles had burned with
the strength of greed and it had killed him. Muhi had wanted
to prove his friendship. Fhrel had insisted and Nerva had
thought it a game.

Gone. Failures all.

Could he have done better?

Even so he should have tried. Should still try—was he to
wait and die while thinking of making the attempt?

"No, Gustav! No!" This time it was the woman who had
read his thoughts. She reached out and took him by the
shoulders and turned him to face her and she did it as if he
were a child. "No," she said again. "I've given the orders and
you couldn't even if you tried. And I don't want you to try.
Haven't I lost enough as it is? Dear God, haven't I lost
enough!"

Too much and all that made life a meaningful existence.
He must reassure her and give her hope.

"We'll find a way," he said. "We can send to other worlds
for experts. To Payne and to—" He broke off, looking at the
hand she had pressed over his heart. "Kathryn?"

"I've been a fool, Gustav. To have put my hope in a monk
and then to be so disappointed when he failed to perform a
miracle. Then to come to you and upset you in turn. But
there must be no stupid heroics. That is an order. I mustn't
lose you, too." She waited until he met her eyes. "I want you
to promise. I want you to give me your word."

A moment and then he nodded. "You have it."

"Good." She inhaled and then stepped back away from
him again in full emotional control. "Thank you, husband."

"You will stay?"

"I can't." She saw regret in his eyes and hastened to explain. "I've work to be getting on with. A stupid bitch who

is too ambitious for her own good needs to be taught a
lesson. I want everything arranged."

The pens were washed and clean but for reasons of hygi-
ene not comfort. The same reasoning applied to the floor, the
walls, the catwalk on which the slaves were displayed, the
block on which they were sold. Only the seats provided for
the curious were padded; serious buyers preferred to stand.

Maureen Clairmont had been among them. She was gone
now, leaving tight-lipped and with the skin stretched tautly
over her cheekbones, realizing just on the edge of ruin the
plan which had been devised against her. One only the Matriarch herself could have engineered, as her backers must realize; and, knowing the strength of the displayed opposition,
they would be quick to disavow her.

Leaning back in her chair, Kathryn felt the glow of satisfaction of a job well done.

"Twenty males," said the auctioneer. "Assorted planets of
origin. Offered for sale by Hylda Vroom. I will allow the
usual time for examination."

A man who relished his power over others but one who
knew how to be deferential while maintaining his pride. Not
an easy thing to do while selling others of his own kind but
such work was too demeaning for any woman to contem-
plate. As the line shuffled from the pens to stand on the catwalk Kathryn leaned forward to study them the better. As
the auctioneer had said, they were a motley crew dressed in
an assortment of garments. A convenience; why provide fresh
clothing when there was no need? And why heat a compart-
ment when clothing would keep the captives warm?

They would have been searched, naturally, and all of value
taken. And, equally naturally, some showed the signs of combat.

And yet was that wholly natural?

To Shamarre who attended her Kathryn said, "Isn't gas
used during a raid?"

"Yes, my lady."

"Then why are some of those men hurt? Is Hylda so careless as to stacking? Or did she have trouble once in space?"

"Trouble," said Shamarre with relish. "You're looking at
the fruit of a couple of raids, my lady. The second proved
expensive. Some managed to escape the gas and decided to

fight. That one, you see him? The one in gray? I heard that he killed a score on his own."

An exaggeration, it had to be, no man could best a score of women especially if they were armed and alert. Yet there was something about him that attracted her interest. His height for one thing, he was taller than Gustav and far wider across the shoulders, but it wasn't just that. His face held a hard, ruthless determination, his eyes probing the area even as he was urged toward the block. On the side of his head an ugly wound made a patch of red and blue which set off the taut pallor of his face.

She lifted her hand as the auctioneer began his chant.

"One moment. I would like some details as to this man."

"My lady?"

"Details, you fool," snapped Shamarre. "Where was he taken? How did he get hurt?"

"I can answer that." Hilda Vroom, gaudy in her flared and slashed blouse, the bulk of an electronic control box at her waist, thrust herself toward the Matriarch. "He comes from Onorldi—at least that's where we found him. I'll be honest, Abra was a fool. Somehow he and others escaped the gas and she hesitated before taking action. While he provided a distraction the rest managed to get weapons and attacked the rafts. We didn't know the situation and so had to make a run for it." She added bitterly, "We left twenty behind."

"Twenty!" Shamarre blew out her cheeks. "You admit it?"

"Why lie? It wasn't my responsibility. I wasn't in command then. We had him surrounded and then, somehow, everyone was firing at everyone else. But I know for a fact he killed a half a dozen and injured more."

"With a gun?"

"A gun and this." Light glittered from the blade of the knife she pulled from her belt. "I'm keeping it for a souvenir."

Shamarre held out her hand and grunted as she examined the weapon. As she handed it back she said, "I still can't understand how you let him get so many of you."

"He's fast. I was on the raft watching and one second he was standing apparently harmless and the next he'd cut loose." She added defensively, "You don't have to believe me. I don't give a damn if you do or don't. You wanted the facts and I'm giving them to you. That's all."

"Dangerous?"

"Not now." The slaver slapped the box at her waist. "I've got him collared."

Kathryn could see it around his throat, the thick band of flexible links shining with a gilt luster. Too close-fitting to be slipped over the head it would detonate if removed with any other means than the correct key. The device incorporated within would respond to signals sent from the slaver's box and turn nerve and muscle into liquid fire should the man disobey.

For a moment she wondered what it must be like to be rendered so helpless. To be dependent on the slightest whim of another. To live in constant fear of pain and death. To be so much a helpless prisoner. A moment in which to taste a foreign concept and to reject it as being totally inapplicable to her situation. She was a woman and the Matriarch. How could she find any affinity with a man and a slave?

"He's big," murmured Shamarre. "And looks strong enough to earn his keep. Gelded, he'd be safe enough to put over the youngsters."

A hint? Shamarre was rarely subtle but what she said was true enough. Young daughters of the aristocracy needed to be taught and protected, and keeping them in line posed a problem. Older women would intrigue and were not above yielding to passions of their own. Men were men. Slaves, unless of a special kind, could be suborned. Loyalty, she thought bitterly. Always it came to that. How to win it? How to keep it once given?

But, from a slave, at least she could ensure obedience. The box Hylda carried would see to that.

"His name?" She nodded as it was given. "Dumarest. Earl Dumarest. And not a native of Onorldi?"

"I doubt it, my lady."

As she did. This man was no farmer spending his life in devotion to the soil. No herder of beasts. No scrap of living matter adjusting his life to the turn of the seasons. There was a proud arrogance to the lift of his head, a savage independence in his eyes. Things she could appreciate even while deploring them in a slave.

"Have him walk," she commanded. "I want to see him move."

As a slaver turned, she rose to step down toward the catwalk. As the order was given, she halted and looked up to study the taut pallor of the face, the inflamed ugliness of the wound.

"A near miss, my lady," said Shamarre at her side. "The bullet must have cracked his skull. There could be inflammation of the inner membranes. Mention it—it will help to lower the price."

The woman was incorrigible, surely she knew that the Matriarch did not haggle like a merchant, yet she had a point. Such an injury could have turned the man into a shambling idiot.

"Have him move," she ordered. "Twist and bend and flex his arms. I want to be certain as to his coordination."

"'You heard!" Hylda dropped her hand to the box at her waist. "Obey, you scum!"

Dumarest felt the first sear of pain as her hand tightened on the control and turned, moving as he'd been directed, but deliberataely slow and awkward. He saw the look of distaste in the woman's eyes. Saw the older woman standing just behind her shake her head and knew he had gone a little too far. Pausing, he sucked in his breath and lifted a hand to press at his wound.

"I apologize, my lady," he said. "I am clumsy, but it will pass. With your permission I will attempt to do better."

An intelligent man and one with at least a touch of culture. His tone had been respectful and his form of address calculated to cause no offense. A pity about the wound.

"Does it hurt?" Kathryn stepped a little closer to the edge of the catwalk. "The wound—does it cause pain?"

"Yes, my lady."

"And your vision? Can you see well?"

"At times it blurs and I see double." Dumarest extended his arms and swept his fingers together. The tips met only after the second attempt. "You see? But I am getting better."

"Liar!" Hylda twisted the control and looked in fury at the strained, sweating figure crouched on the catwalk. A long moment during which she enjoyed the spectacle then, remembering risked profit, cut the stimulus and allowed peace to come to tormented sinews. "You are fit and know it. Now stop this stupid pretense and act normal."

Dumarest said nothing, looking at his hands, seeing the skin stretched taut over the knuckles, feeling the sweat dew-

ing his face and neck and running in little rivulets over his
body. Waiting to master his weakness, to shield the hate in
his eyes, to rise at last, to stagger a little and stand like a
dumb, helpless beast.

Shamarre said flatly, "What was that supposed to prove,
Hylda? That he is made of flesh and bone? Or do you believe
that if you beat a dog hard enough it will learn to talk?"

"The man is a slave and is still my property. I do with him
as I please."

Hylda had stepped closer the better to watch his pain and
now stood barely nine feet from Dumarest. The Matriarch
was a little farther and to one side, her guard a pace more
distant. Others, lounging in the seats, watched with casual interest. The auctioneer. waiting to commence the bidding,
made a point of appearing to be unconcerned. No other
slaves were close.

With sudden decision Kathryn said, "I will buy him. Have
him healed and gelded and delivered to the palace."

As she turned to walk away Dumarest moved.

A leap and he was before the slaver, one hand lifted to
send the stiffened fingers stabbing into the soft flesh of her
throat, his other snatching the knife from where she carried it
in her belt. Even as she screamed he drove it forward, sending it to penetrate the control box at her waist, electronic
energy sparking as the steel plunged, twisted, destroying the
inner components as it passed through to reach the flesh of
her stomach, to slice into skin and fat and muscle, to release
the intestines in a shower of blood and inner fluids.

Even as she died he was moving again, this time to reach
the Matriarch, to send his left arm looping over her shoulder,
to hold her close as his right hand weighted with the blood-
stained blade lifted the knife to press against her throat.

"Hold!" His voice blasted an inch from her ear. "Freeze or
she dies!"

Stunned, unbelieving, Shamarre stepped forward still unable to grasp the situation. It had all happened so fast! A
matter of seconds during which the slaver had been killed
and her mistress taken hostage.

"You swine! Harm her and—"

"Back!" Dumarest met her eyes, his naked fury halting her
instinctive advance. "Back or she dies!" The knife moved in
his hand, turning so as to rest the smeared point against the

white column of the trapped throat. A pressure and the jugular would be severed.

And he would do it. Staring at him Shamarre had no doubt as to that. A savage, desperate man with nothing to lose. One who knew how to handle weapons and who was not a stranger to death. One who at this moment was ready to end his life.

"A warning," he said. "If anyone tries to activate my collar I'll plunge this knife home. At the first touch of pain she dies. And if you detonate it she goes with me. Now get me the key. You!" He glared at Shamarre. "Get me the key!"

It was inside Hylda's pouch and even as she found it the woman knew why Dumarest had wasted no time searching for it. The hostage had to come first—with the Matriarch in his power he was safe for the moment and the thought gave her relief. A desperate man, yes, but one still able to plan consciously. To struggle for the life she thought he was ready to yield. Which meant that he would be reluctant to commit the final act which would lead to his inevitable extinction.

"Here!" She stepped toward him, the key in her hand. "Shall I—"

"Throw it!"

A move and the knife was in his left hand as his right snatched the key from the air. Blindly he fumbled with the glittering band, his fingers searching for the tiny keyhole. Finding it, he slipped the key inside, took a breath and twisted. The key fit, the collar did not explode, and he flung it from him to lie like a gleaming serpent in the puddle of the slaver's blood.

"And now?" Kathryn shared his relief. "You've got rid of the collar but how does that help you?'"

"One thing at a time." Dumarest looked about the room. By this time, unless the place was totally staffed by hysterical fools, there would be guards waiting and ready to pounce. "If you gave me your word could I trust it?"

"Of course. I am the Matriarch of Esslin."

And a proud woman who would not easily forgive this insult. And one who could not be kept a prisoner indefinately. Even now she must be planning on how best to make a break. To risk the knife in the certain knowledge that, once beyond his reach, she would be safe. And she needn't even do that. Marksmen, correctly stationed, could burn him down without harming the woman.

"It seems that you are in a rather difficult position," she said dryly. "I can understand your desire to get rid of the collar, and the slaver was no loss, but what now?"

"We go on a journey."

"To the field?" She was shrewd. "Hylda's vessel? How can you be sure the crew will accommodate you?"

A gamble he had to take. The only chance he had. And he could afford to waste no time.

"We're leaving, my lady," he said quietly. "It would be wise for you to give me full cooperation. That way neither of us will get hurt."

"And if I struggle or appeal for help or anything like that which threatens you then you will kill me. Is that it?"

"Not kill you. Not if I can avoid it." He left the threat unspoken but the sting of the knife was enough. "Now lead the way out. Keep close and . . . and . . . ." He blinked, looking at her face which seemed to waver. And then, suddenly, there was nothing.

Chapter Three

"Slaver gas." Gustav Acchabaron lifted his goblet and studied the wine within. "A compound designed to serve a specific purpose and I think you will admit most useful in certain emergencies."

"Such as the release of a hostage?"

"Certainly." Gustav sipped then lowered his goblet. "But come, Earl, you aren't eating and the physicians tell me that nourishment is essential after treatment with slow-time. Incidentally, how is the head?"

Healed, the wound nothing but a trace of scar tissue beneath the cover of his hair, the internal inflammation cured in a matter of hours during which he had lain unknowing and unconscious as drugs had accelerated his metabolism. Slow-time which had compressed the hours so that he'd had the benefit of long, natural healing.

And stranger still had been his welcome after waking.

Leaning back Dumarest looked at the chamber to which he had been guided, the man who was his host. The husband of the Matriarch who, in such a society, would take a minor part in public affairs. Private ones too if the culture followed the patterns of others he had known. Yet the man, for all his apparent show of kindness, was being cruel.

Dumarest said flatly, "What is my position now?"

"You are my guest."

"And?"

"You expect retribution?" Gustav shook his head and smiled. "I am remiss but you must remember that days have passed since the gas rendered you unconscious. Time in which things have been decided. Time too for anger to cool. The Lady Kathryn is a firm ruler but not a sadistic one. She would not allow you to be plied with wines and viands before your execution. She would consider it a waste."

36

"She would be right." Dumarest helped himself to more meat and ate it, chewing well before swallowing, merely wetting his lips with the wine. Gustav could be honest and mean what he said but he did not rule. "Your wife, my lord, is a most unusual woman."

"You think so?"

Dumarest nodded, remembering the hard lines of the body he had held, the firmness beneath the clothing. She had never, at any time, displayed fear. She had made no attempt to struggle, knowing it was useless. She had made no threats or protestations and she had offered no bribes.

And now, for some incredible reason of her own, she had spared his life.

And spared his neck the weight of a collar.

Gustav saw the lift of Dumarest's hand to his throat and guessed the thought behind the gesture.

"You taught her something," he said quietly. "No man should wear a collar such as that."

"Nor should anyone be a slave."

"True."

"You agree? And yet you tolerate it?"

"I tolerate what I must." Gustav drank wine, remembering, finding no pleasure in the memories. "We are all the victims of our culture, Earl. On Esslin slavery is common. An ancient tradition which has been maintained and it has all the strength of established habit. The fields must be tended and the crops harvested and who else is to do the work if not slaves?"

"Machines. Free men and women. Paid workers."

"So I have argued. I know that slavery is uneconomic and inefficient aside from being inhumane. I know too that those who buy slaves are worse than those who raid for them, for without a market such creatures would cease to exist. But logic and sense have little weight against rooted conviction and there are few who dare to stand against the present order of things." Gustav helped himself to more wine. "It is a pleasure to talk to a man like yourself. You are a breath of fresh wind tearing away cobwebs. A man who has traveled far and seen much. Neiras, perhaps? Subik? Anchayha?"

Names lost among a mass of others and all to the forgotten. Planets and worlds which spun about their suns and with each revolution falling farther into the past. Points on a seemingly endless journey which had merged to form a pattern illuminated by violence and blood and pain and aching loss.

"No," said Dumarest. "I know none of the worlds you mention."

"But others?"

"Others, yes.'"

"Many like Esslin?"

Too many. Small worlds with limited areas and scant populations. Static cultures frozen in ancient moulds with the dead hand of long-established expediency stifling further growth. Clans, Houses, Families, Tribes—some locked in the maw of Unions and Guilds and none wholly free. Backwaters among the stars. Bad worlds for a traveler on which to land. Some of them almost impossible to leave. Planets on which men starved because they could find no work. Others in which savagery ruled in places, as isolated communes slid back down the ladder of evolution.

Perhaps, somewhere, there was a world which had forged ahead and on which all men were at liberty to make any choice they wished. A truly free world on which liberty and the concept of equality was accepted in the purest sense. One on which no man sought to impose his will on another.

It could exist.

Dumarest had never found it.

"Slavery," mused Gustav. "How did you come to be a slave?"

"Luck."

"Luck?"

"Bad luck. I was at the wrong place at the wrong time. Another day and I wouldn't be sitting here now." Dumarest selected a fruit from a bowl and peeled the scarlet rinds from the crisp flesh of the violet pulp. "What is to happen to me?"

"Now?" Gustav gestured at the table. "You eat and drink and enjoy the moment."

"For tomorrow I die?" Dumarest dropped the fruit and leaned toward his host. "What happens to me when this farce is over?"

"No farce, Earl. But to answer your question, we talk."

"Talk now."

Gustav sighed and moved a scrap of food on his plate

then, as if arriving at a decision, thrust the plate to one side and rested his elbows on the cleared space.

"I will be blunt, Earl. Your position is not good."

"As a slave?"

"That is academic. You have killed. You have attacked the Matriarch and threatened her life. The penalty for such an offense is to be impaled. And I tell you now that unless Kathryn pardons you that is exactly what will happen."

Taken and mounted on a slender point to have it thrust into the space between his thighs then to be left for his own weight to drive it deeper into his body. A long, cruel, lingering death.

"You are being watched," said Gustav quickly. "Even if you kill me it will make no difference. And, unlike the Matriarch, I am of little importance."

Which was why he acted the host. Dumarest forced himself to relax. Now was not the time for action and the mere fact that he had been healed and fed and treated as he was at this moment showed there was hope. But the threat had been real. Of that he had no doubt.

"After the feast, the reckoning," he said. "Well, how much will it be?"

"A journey into hell," said Gustav seriously. "One from which no one has yet returned."

Waiting was a torment and yet there was nothing she could do other than wait. Gustav had insisted and she had to admit his logic in the matter. To demand, to bluster, to threaten—how would that serve if met with stubborn refusal? She could kill, true, but what would that gain? And the chance must not be lost. Never, perhaps, could it be repeated. Against that what was a little time?

Locked in the humming fields of Tamiras's magic Kathryn turned and fought the tension which not even the electronic wizardry could dissolve. To remain idle when so much of importance was at stake!

"My lady?" Shamarre was at her side apparently summoned and yet Kathryn had no memory of calling the woman. Or of wanting her. But now that she was here it would be wise to find something for her to do. An errand to save her pride if nothing else.

"Check with the observers and report as to progress."

Shamarre made no attempt to move. "Progress is as expected, my lady. The initial barrier had been safely passed and the rest should be relatively simple. I must confess I did not think your consort had so much delicacy in him. I know some women who could learn from his tact."

Words! Empty praise! A sop to calm her fears!

"Is that what you came to tell me?"

"There has been another death. From the north. Two victims of hnaudifida have been reported from the adjoining sector."

"Complete restriction of all movement in the area. Send guards to patrol the boundaries and warn all residents they will shoot to kill if my orders are disobeyed. This applies to citizens as well as slaves."

"Yes, my lady." Shamarre hesitated. "Shall I check with the physicians as to their work on a vaccine?"

"Leave that to me. Do as I have ordered. Move!"

Now, at least, she had something to do and an excuse for visiting the laboratories. A genuine one and Gustav would have no reason to think that she was checking up on him, doubting his ability to perform the task they had agreed should be his alone. A wise decision, she hoped, and his arguments had carried weight. But if anything should happen to him. If Dumarest should turn out to be even more violent and savage than she had guessed then his death would not be easy. There were worse things than impalement.

"My lady!" The technician bowed. "You were not expected and the Director is with your consort and his companion. A moment and I will summon her."

"Never mind." The girl was trying too hard to please. "Where are they? The compound? No, don't bother to guide me. I know where it is."

A place set deep within the building and shielded for always against the sun. A circular area some hundred yards across capped with a domed roof now glowing with a soft emerald to emulate the natural sky. The floor was of polished stone patterned in a wild variety of flowers and benches ran around the walls. Mirrors had been set in them, planes of reflective glass graced with pastoral scenes, but Dumarest didn't look at them, guessing them to be more than they seemed.

Instead he looked at the creature who shambled in a continuous circle in the center of the compound.

Once he had been young and good looking with strong bones and square-set shoulders and lips which smiled to show flashing teeth and hair which framed a strongly-boned face with an ebon aureole. A tall, lithe athlete proud of his trained and harnessed skills. A man able to run and jump and wrestle.

Now a man without a mind.

A caricature which drooled as it moved and moved as if muscle and bone had been warped and distorted into alien configurations. A thing which had no control over its bodily functions.

"Muhi," said Gustav quietly. "A friend. There are others and some of them are worse than what you see. None is better. Some have died. None have recovered."

"Treatment?"

"The best available. Skilled psychologists and trained practitioners of the mental arts. Even a monk of the Church of Universal Brotherhood. All have failed."

"To treat the symptoms or the cause?" Dumarest stepped toward the shambling figure and halted before it. As it neared he placed both hands on the rounded shoulders and pressed as he stared into the eyes. They were vague, the pupils dilated, the balls rolling, shifting in a continual refusal to focus on any one object. For a moment Dumarest maintained the position then, dropping his hands, he stepped back. "Drugs?"

"We have tried them all. Sedatives, tranquilizers, stimulants, herbs and elaborate compounds. Even charms and spells."

"Alcohol?" Have you tried getting him drunk?"

"What good would that do?"

"Alcohol is a depressant. If his condition is due to hyperactivity of the synapses then slowing that activity could show an improvement." Dumarest suddenly swung his fist at the patient's face, halting it a fraction from the skin. "No reaction. He seems to be in a totally different world."

"He is."

Mentally, of course, but that was enough. Watching the shambling movements, Dumarest could sense the alien atmosphere the man emitted, a strangeness as if he were something other than human. That continual flicker of the eyes as if he were impelled to watch the darting motion of a heated

molecule or the random flight of an insect. The odor which
he exuded. The odd configuration of his limbs.

Muhi, a friend so Gustav had said—what if he had been
an enemy?

To the Director he said, "What is your opinion as to the
cause?"

"A progressive breakdown of the autonomic functions,"
she said without hesitation. As you must be aware, many
physical operations are conducted without the need for mental directives. For example we breathe and blink our eyes
without conscious direction. Our hearts beat without voluntary directives. Our digestion, liver functions and so on work
as a near-automatic unit. This attribute has given rise to the
theory that the body has a subconscious life of its own on a
basic primeval level. I think this assumption is false and what
we have seen tends to prove it. The patient no longer has
mental control and his physical body is suffering from accumulated errors which would normally have been corrected
by the mental process. Think of a machine," she suggested.
"One which runs perfectly for a while without attendance but
which, if left too long, will become erratic because minor
faults aren't checked early enough."

"Like the flight computer in a ship," said Dumarest. "It
bases its program on received information but can deliver
some pretty wild figures unless checks are made to erase accumulated garbage. A correct analogy?"

"Yes."

"And you can't erase the garbage?"

She frowned and glanced at Gustav, who shrugged.

"We aren't dealing with a machine," she said stiffly. "The
patient is a human being."

"Is he?" Dumarest met her eyes. "How far does he have to
go before he ceases to be that? I didn't see a man just then. I
saw a lost animal. If anything of the original man remains it
is frightened and hiding. Where, Director? Where could it
hide? What section of the brain can it run to?" Then, before
she could reply he said, "A serious question this time. What
would you say is the breaking point of a man like the patient? How far can he be pressed before his mind will snap?"

"I don't know," she said. "I doubt if anyone could answer
that with any degree of certainty. There are too many varia-
bles. A coward can display unexpected courage in times of

stress. An apparently brave person can panic for no obvious cause. Heroines are born of the moment."

"But all are subject to weaknesses?"

"Of course."

"Do the patients have any in common? Did they all have a fear of falling, for example, or of fire?"

"I know what you mean. The answer is not as far as we are aware."

"You checked?"

"No," she admitted. "Not before it was too late to make personal examination in depth. Even then the results could have been negative. Some fears are so deeply buried they only surface beneath the impact of extreme stimuli." To Gustav she said, "Are there any further questions?"

"Earl?"

Dumarest shook his head and watched as the woman left, the patient with her. Quietly he said, "Was Muhi a traveler on that journey you mentioned?"

"Yes."

"And the others?"

"Yes," said Gustav again and felt relief now that it was out. "Volunteers, all of them, heroes each and every one."

"Heroes?"

"You probably think of them as fools. But to me they are heroes. Brave men who took a terrible risk and were willing to pay the price if they failed. Well, they did fail. Somehow they weren't strong enough and now they are dying. Soon they will all be dead." Gustav glanced at the mirrors, wondering behind which Kathryn would be standing. Knowing she had to be there, watching, hoping. Knowledge which prompted him to add, "As you will be dead unless you are willing to cooperate."

Dumarest said dryly, "You offer me a poor choice. Death in one way or death in another. Looking at your friend I think I'd prefer to be your enemy."

"You refuse!"

"To walk blindly into a trap, yes. To take a chance with the prospect of reward is another matter. You offer a reward?"

"Isn't your life—" Gustav broke off then continued, "There will be a reward if you are successful. That I promise. And it

will be large. The Matriarch will be generous to the man who
restores her daughter to a normal life."

"Her daughter?"

"And mine." Gustav looked at the mirrors. "Our only
child."

"Iduna," said Kathryn. "We named her Iduna. It was a
name found by Gustav in an old book."

"One a trader brought me, Earl. The name is that of an
ancient goddess of spring, the guardian of the golden apples
which the gods tasted whenever they wished to restore their
youth."

"Legend."

"Of course, but what of that? And surely you have no
quarrel with legend? A man who dreams of finding Earth?"
Gustav smiled and gestured with both hands. "A scrap of delirium, Earl. You raved a little as they operated on your
wound. Nonsense, naturally, but interesting as a matter of
speculation. Mysterious planets, lost and forgotten which offer tremendous riches to those who are fortunate enough to
find them. Earth is but one. Paradise is another. Eden another, I think, and Bonanza too if I am not mistaken. I have
a list here somewhere."

"Leave it," said Kathryn as he turned to rummage among
his papers. "We have other things to discuss."

They were in Gustav's study where she had joined them together with wine. Glasses to ease the tension and to occupy
hands, though Dumarest needed no such aids. A mistake, she
thought, the careful manipulation had been unnecessary. A
direct proposition would have worked just as well but it had
seemed wise to be sure. And she had doubted her own reaction to his presence. Anger, aroused at memory of his touch,
his threats could have overwhelmed her. Even now she had to
remember that he was to be used and was worth more alive
than dead. Remembering that she held his life in her hands
helped her to retain her equanimity. And she needed him. If
he could win where the others had failed all would be forgiven.

The wine slopped in her glass as she lifted it to her lips
and drank, barely tasting the wine, feeling only its needed
warmth.

"Iduna," said Dumarest meeting her eyes. "Your daughter who is lost."

"Not lost. Not exactly. That is—Gustav, why don't you explain?"

"You saw the man in the compound," he said. "Would you say he was lost?"

"In a manner of speaking, yes."

"And Iduna is lost in a similar way. That is we have her body safe on Esslin. We even know what happened to her. We can guess where her mind, her intelligence must be. But we can't find it, Earl. We can't get to her. We can't guide her back to us!"

A mystery. Dumarest waited for him to explain.

"I collect old things." Gustav gestured toward his desk, the crammed files standing against the wall, the shelves holding enigmatic objects. "Traders bring them knowing of my interest and usually they ask little for what, to them, is rubbish. To others too, perhaps, but to me it is an entrancing hobby. To piece scraps together to form a whole, to build from it, to guess and surmise, to indulge in fantasy and explore myths such as that of Earth. It began when, as a boy, I was given an old almanac. Then a recording of a play in which strange names were used. I've them both somewhere and used to value them highly. Now I wish to God I'd never seen them!"

The man was distraught. Dumarest poured wine and handed him the goblet.

"Thank you," Gustav drank and sucked in his breath. "I digress. Iduna, I must tell you about Iduna. Of the thing she found while I was away. That damned, cursed thing found on a blighted world!"

"Gustav!"

"Yes." He looked at the woman, responding to the iron note of command. "Yes, my dear."

"You were not to blame!"

"So you tell me. But if it hadn't been for my interest. If I had been more careful. If I hadn't—"

"Luck," said Dumarest. "We spoke about it, remember? Bad luck which causes you to do the wrong thing at the wrong time. The kind which made me a victim of slavers." He glanced at the woman. "Which almost cost me my life."

Without looking at him she said, "Continue, Gustav."

"A thing," he said. "A trader bought it, he said, and

thought of me. If he told the truth about its origins it was found when an earth-mover dug up a mass of debris and dropped it on the surface. The story could be true, stranger things have happened, and at the time I wasn't interested. The thing itself was enough. An artifact of some kind and one never made by man. You realize what I am saying, Earl? I held the product of an alien civilization in my hands."

Dumarest wasn't impressed. "In some sectors such things are common. Bricks fashioned by some ant-like creature with rudimentary intelligence. Pots made of dust cemented with spittle. Discs scored with lines which could be equations of some kind. And—"

"Rubbish!" Gustav was impatient. "I know of such items and they prove nothing but that certain life forms constructed certain patterns which need have nothing to do with true intelligence. But can you deny that others must have lived in the galaxy before us?"

"No."

"Then you can understand my excitement. I had examined it in a dozen ways and finally gained a response to certain stimuli. A reaction which registered on a dozen instruments. I couldn't wait. I ran to the laboratory to gain the aid of experts and, while I was gone, Iduna entered the study."

Memory of it made him weak, events long past suddenly alive again so that he could hear the thud of his feet as he ran, instinct warning him something was wrong. Feel again the pounding of his heart, the empty sickness in his stomach, the shouts which tore his throat, the tears which stung his eyes.

See again the small, limp figure lying before the damned artifact.

A sacrifice to his alien god.

"Here!" He looked up and saw Dumarest standing close with a glass in his hand. Dutifully he took it and drank and coughed as the contents caught at his throat. Brandy this time, distilled energy, an anodyne to the pain which had been obvious for all with eyes to see. "And then?"

"Nothing!" The glass shattered in his hand and he stared at the blood marring the whiteness of his palm. "Nothing!"

Nothing but endless grief, endless regret, the hollow emptiness and the accusation, never admitted, which he saw in

Kathryn's eyes. Or imagined he saw—what did it matter? The guilt was his.

"We tried," said Kathryn. "My technicians aren't fools and it was obvious the collapse had to be connected somehow with the Tau." She noticed Dumarest's frown. "We had to call it something."

"Isn't the word connected with something precious?"

"Anything connected with my daughter is that. But as I was saying tests were made on the Tau and others made on Iduna. She seemed to be asleep but for no apparent cause. No trace of drugs, injury, shock or the passage of any kind of energy. It just seemed that, somehow, she had been sucked from her body. Her awareness, that is, her basic self."

"A working hypothesis," said Gustav. "We had to begin somewhere."

And later facts had supported it. Dumarest listened as they were enumerated, the checks, tests with beasts, tests with the girl, and then, after a long while, the first volunteer.

"He was mad," said Kathryn. "Insane. He had to be to plunge into the unknown. But I think he loved me and certainly he loved my child." She paused then said softly, "He was the first to die."

"How?" Dumarest snapped his impatience. "Save the wake until later, my lady, grief for those I have never known is a luxury I cannot afford. How did the hero die?"

His insult worked as he'd intended. The flush on her cheeks matched the sudden flare of anger in her eyes and, at that moment, she would cheerfully have watched him die. Then Gustav, more perceptive, said, "Earl is right, my dear. He needs to know."

"He died," she said stiffly. "Quickly, thank God, but he taught us a little even as he did so. The next lasted longer and after him came others. You've seen one of the latest."

"And you want me to join them?"

"No! No, Earl, the very opposite." Gustav was emphatic. "We want you to succeed where they failed. To go after Iduna wherever she might be, to find her, to bring her back to us. And, if you do that—"

"Freedom," said Kathryn. "Full citizen status, land, money, slaves if you want them."

And death should he refuse. Dumarest glanced at the litter of papers, the files, the shelves then at the faces of the others.

The man would be reluctant but not the woman. And she had the power.

"Well?"

"Iduna," said Dumarest. "It's time that I saw her."

The room was a womb, a place in which to hold a precious egg, the walls of softly shimmering satin, the floor piled with sterile whiteness. The bed was long and wide and as starkly white as the rest of the furnishings. On it, covered by a single sheet, rested a girl.

She was small, delicately boned, fashioned with an elfin grace. The face was pert, the chin pointed, the eyes closed, lashes lying like resting moths on the smooth alabaster of her cheeks. Beneath the cover her body held an immature softness. Hair spilled from her rounded skull to frame her face with a tapestry of jet.

Dumarest had expected a child. He saw a young and lovely girl.

"She was eleven when it happened," whispered Gustav. "That was years ago now. She has grown since then."

Fed by machines, massaged by devoted servants, her physical well-being monitored every moment of the day. Dumarest could see the thin lines of monitor wires, the staring eyes of electronic alarms.

"Does she move?"

"At times, yes. Turning as if dreaming in her sleep. At first, during such times, we hoped she was about to recover but always we were disappointed. Now we have almost ceased to hope."

"The others who followed her, did they follow the same pattern?"

"For a while but never for long. Deterioration was present almost from the first. They would fall and seem to be asleep but then display symptoms of unease. Then, when they woke, they were not whole. You've seen Muhi. You know what I mean."

Struggling back to a parody of life to shamble like mindless beasts as their bodies spun into dissolution. The men but not the girl. She had lain quietly for years without apparent harm. Her sex?

"No," said Gustav when Dumarest asked the question. "It can't be that. We had a few female volunteers in the early days but they failed as did the men. And the technicians assure me there is no difference in the structure of a male and female brain."

"We are retreading old ground," said Kathryn. "Let us see the Tau."

It was close, housed in an adjoining chamber, one which had been enlarged to hold a battery of instruments and testing devices all centered on the alien thing which stood at chest height on a stand of polished rods. A light shone down on it, a cone of harsh, white brilliance balanced by others focused from ground level so as to eliminate all shadow.

A thing double the size of a man's head, rounded, nodulated, alien—and beautiful!

Dumarest walked toward it, seeing the shimmering interplay of light on the granulated surface, the birth and death of living rainbows, wells of luminescence which winked and shifted to glow again and to vanish as the eye attempted to examine their configurations.

Light from the focused brilliance caught and reflected into breathtaking splendor.

Or was it just the light?

Dumarest said, not turning his head, "Is this the usual arrangement? Are things as they were when the volunteers took their chance?"

Kathryn said, "Marita?"

The technician was old, her face smooth, her hair a crested mass of silver, yet there was nothing soft or weak about her eyes and nothing indecisive in her voice.

"Things are exactly the same, my lady."

"Speak to Dumarest. Answer his questions. Explain if he needs explanations."

"Facts will do." He stared into the woman's eyes and saw the reflected glow of the cones of brilliance, the sparkling shimmer of the Tau. "Always it is the same?"

"There have been variations. We are not fools. Temperatures have ranged from freezing to half again the heat of blood. There has been calculated vibration and electronic blankets of silence. It is all in the reports."

"I've no time to read them. Turn off the lights." Dumarest looked again at the Tau as, reluctantly, she obeyed. The rainbows had not died. The coruscations of color seemed even brighter than before, sparkling and whirling, spinning, holding, expanding to contract to expand again in an attention-holding succession of enticement. "Lights!"

He narrowed his eyes as they blazed into life and turned from the enigmatic object they illuminated. After-images danced to form shifting blurs of color, and he waited until they had gone. From across the room a technician studying monitors coughed and swallowed, the sound oddly loud.

"Well?" Marita was looking at him. She radiated the impatience of an expert to one who had interloped into her field. "Is there anything else?"

"Did the volunteers take any precautions? Make any preparations?"

"What would be the point? Clothing and weapons would be useless."

"I was thinking of less tangible things. Appeals to the gods, perhaps. Prayers. Mental adjustments of some kind. Deep breathing, even." His voice hardened. "I'm serious, woman!"

"Some, yes," she admitted. "They would vocalize their mental attitudes. Others seemed to meditate before taking the final step. You know what that is, of course?"

"I know what it has to be."

"Then—"

"That will be all. Thank you for your courtesy." He looked at Gustav. "Did Iduna often play with the things she found in your study?"

"Yes."

"There was no rule against it? No prohibition she could be conscious of breaking?"

"No, of course not. Why do you ask? What are you getting at?"

Questions Dumarest ignored as he stood thinking, remembering, assessing the information he had gained. It was little enough but it would have to do.

"The time," he said. "When you found Iduna in your study what time was it?"

"Late afternoon." Gustav sounded baffled. "Earl, I don't understand what you are getting at. What does the time matter?"

"You have only one window and the sun sets to one side. Am I correct?"

"Yes. The window faces to the north and the sun sets in the west." Sudden understanding warmed the man's voice.

"The light? You think the intensity of light had something to do with it?"

"Perhaps. Marita, lower the brilliance of the lights." Dumarest frowned as they died. "Don't kill them, woman! Just dim them."

"How? We have no rheostat in the circuit."

"Then fit one!" Kathryn was sharp. "And be quick about it!" As the technician hurried to obey she said to Dumarest, "You have discovered something? You have a plan?"

"An idea. It may be nothing." He knew she wanted more. "A question of attitude," he explained. "I feel it could be important."

"Is that all?" She frowned her disappointment, the frown clearing as Marita called that all was ready. The woman had worked fast. "Have you seen enough?"

Dumarest nodded. The gamble had to be taken, there was no point in extending delay.

"Then commence!"

Guards stepped from where they had been lurking in the shadows, armed, armored, strong women dedicated to the Matriarch. Invisible until now but always Dumarest had been conscious of their presence. Watching, waiting for him to move, to make the journey which others had taken and which, for them, had ended in mindless dead. One he had no choice but to take in turn.

"Dim the lights," he ordered. "More. More—keep dimming until you emulate a shadowed room."

The harsh glare faded as he began to walk toward the Tau, dulling even more as the complimentary lights died so as to leave the enigmatic object apparently unsupported and shining with a soft effulgence as if oil had been spread on glowing water.

Dumarest stared at it, concentrating, adjusting his attitude, blanking out the threat of guards and possible horror. Forgetting those who had gone before aside from one. Iduna who now lay quietly sleeping in a room of sterile whiteness.

And, walking, he stepped through time and space to a point years in the past when a happy, carefree child came skipping into a deserted study to discover something new and wonderful which held an immediate fascination. A bright and glowing object illuminated by the dusty light of the setting sun. Enigmatic, mysterious, magical.

And he became that child, running now, entranced, eager to discover what a doting parent had bought. To reach out with open arms. To fold them around the Tau. To hug it close and to press his face against the bright enchantment. To feel the faintest of tingles and to see the luminosity suddenly expand to engulf him. To take him elsewhere.

Chapter Four

He was in a room designed for the use of giants with walls which soared like the face of cliffs and a ceiling which looked like a shadowed sky. The floor was covered with a carpet with a pile so thick it reached to his ankles and all about loomed the bulk of oddly familiar furniture. Turning he studied grotesquely distorted tables, chairs, something which could have been a desk, something else which held stuffed and sagging dolls.

"Hello, there! Will you play with me?"

Dumarest spun to see a waddling shape come hopping toward him. A parody of what a human should be; the face round as were the eyes, the mouth a grinning slit, the chin merging into the neck, the whole dressed in a clown's attire.

"Will you play?" The voice had a high-pitched squeakiness. "I know lots of fine games. We could hunt the slipper or find the parcel or we could roll marbles or climb. Don't you want to play?"

"Who are you?"

"I'm Clownie. I'm the one who makes you smile when you are sad and unless I am very, very good, *very good*, you give me no tea but that isn't often because always I am good."

"Tea?"

"Tisane. See? Tee for tisane. Tea. Isn't it fun to make up words?"

"Where are we?"

"In Magic Land. Where you always go when you're alone. Now hurry and meet Bear."

Bear was as tall, covered in short brown fur, nose and lips of black, eyes round and gleaming. A wide ribbon adorned his neck and his voice was deep and a little gruff as befitted a serious person.

53

Solemnly he held out a paw. "You are welcome to join me in a game. What shall it be? Soldiers?"

"For that we need armies."

"We have armies. They are in the boxes but if you call them they will come on parade." The bear glanced at the clown. "He doesn't seem to know what to do."

"He needs to eat," said the clown. "I'll get the cakes and you call the others. Hurry, now."

They came from nowhere, oddly shaped creatures of garish colors and peculiar appearance. Eyes and heads and faces seemed alien and yet totally familiar. They moved and talked and aped the style of humans but they were not and could never have been fashioned in human form. They were more like caricatures of familiar types; the fat one with the round, shining face, the fox-like one, the pigs, the toad, the nodding, weaving monkey, the solemn policeman with his truncheon, the giggling girl, the staid matron—the playmates of a lonely child.

Dolls!

Companions of the mind created from the toys of childhood when imagination took things of rag and wood and stuffing and gave them life and form and voices. And the vastness of the room and the furniture.

Dumarest knew the answer.

Leaning back, ignoring the babble around him, he looked at the nursery. The bed would be elsewhere but here, surrounded by comfort, he would play with the toys provided and with the magic of childhood endow them with individual personalities. But he was not a child but a grown man so why should he be in the nursery?

"A cake!" The bear was insistent. "You must have one of these cakes. Mistress Gold baked them and she will be very angry if you do not take one. She may even order you to be shut up in a cupboard for a whole hour. You wouldn't like that, would you?"

"No," said Dumarest.

Then take a cake." The bear nodded as he did so. "And one for you, Clownie. And for you, Foxie. And for you, Toadie." His voice was a drone above the clatter of cups and the ritual of pouring tisane or tea as they called it. A party. A tea party. A pastime beloved by the young, especially young girls who aped their mothers in playing the hostess.

Had Iduna played such games?

Iduna!

Dumarest looked at his cake and set it aside. This was her world, not his. The soft and comfortable world of a loved and cherished child who would find the living toys perfectly natural. A delightful realization of an often-pretended charade in which they would have been placed around the table a   ꞏⁿᵈ tisane and cakes and moved and placed and given words in the entrancing world of make-believe which every child could call his own.

"You dirty thing!" The matron seethed with anger as she glared at one of the pigs. "You spilled tea on my gown! You did it on purpose!"

"It was an accident."

"Don't talk such lies! You should be beaten for having been so bad. Look at my nice new gown! You've spoiled it!"

"Be calm," rumbled the bear. "Ladies, be calm."

"Hit them," suggested the clown to the policeman. "Hit them both."

"Now, now there!" The policeman lurched to his feet. "We don't want trouble, do we?"

"Why not?" The toad gaped and seemed to blur. "Why not?"

The giggling girl half-turned and froze as she lifted her cup to hurl its contents in the face of the red-cheeked drummer who smiled as he toppled to one side to lie with his head in a quivering mass of jelly, his hands still jerking to produce a death-like rattle from his drum.

Anger, the petulance of childish rage had ruined the party but in a moment all could be as before with those involved going through their paces like well-trained puppets manipulated by mental intent. As always during a party when spats and outbursts provided variety. When things were done deserving of punishment which could then be administered with solemn ceremonies.

But this world was not one he had known. His childhood had contained no similar comforts. It had been a time of harsh deprivation unrelieved by moments of joy.

Dumarest shivered, remembering, then shivered again to the chilling wind.

It came from the north where ice still coated the ponds and snow filled the gulleys; the residue of winter stubbornly defying the sun. He glanced at it, narrowing his eyes against the glare, wishing the watery brightness held more strength. Soon it would be dark and all hope of game lost and, again, he would hug an empty belly and nurse bruises from savage blows.

Crouched against the gritty soil he stared at the area ahead. The wind touched his near-naked body, driving knives of ice through the rents, numbing the flesh and blood and causing his teeth to chatter. He clamped them shut, feeling the jerk of muscles in his jaw, the taste of blood as his teeth caught at the tender membranes of his cheeks. Weakness blurred his vision so that the scrub barely masking the stoney ground danced and spun in wild sarabands of bewildering complexity. Impatiently he squeezed shut his eyes, opening them to see the landscape steady again, seeing too the twitch of leaves at the base of a matted bunch of vegetation.

The lizaard was cautious. It thrust its snout from the leaves and stared with unwinking eyes before making a small dart forward to freeze again as it checked its surroundings for possible enemies. Watching it, Dumarest forced himself to freeze.

To rise now would be to lose the prey; it would dive into cover at the first sign of movement. Only later, after it had come into the open to warm itself by the weak sunlight and search for grubs, would he have a chance and then only one. For now he must wait as the wind chilled his body, gnawing at him with spiteful teeth, sending more pain to join the throb of old bruises, the sores from festering wounds, the ache of hunger and fatigue.

He narrowed his eyes as the wind lifted dust and threw it into his face, stirring the lank mane of his hair and fluttering the ragged neck of his single garment. A movement which would have scared the quarry had it not been out of its sight and the wind carried his scent from the reptile who, moving with greater assurance now, had come well into the open.

Dumarest flexed his fingers and touched the crude sling at his side. A leather pouch and thongs made from the hides of small rodents. Stones carefully selected and of the size of small eggs. He would have time for one cast only—if he missed the chance would be lost. All depended on choosing the exact moment, of hand and arm and eye working in harmony, of speed which would enable him to strike before the lizard could run to safety.

Now?

The creature was alerted, head lifted, eyes like jewels as they caught and reflected the sunlight, scaled body blending with the soil on which it stood. It would be best to wait.

To wait as the wind chilled his blood and stiffened his muscles, as dirt stung his eyes and the sickening fear that he might miss added itself to the destructive emotions of his being. Then, guided by subconscious dictates, to act. To rise, the loaded sling lifting, to swing in a sharp circle, the thong released at the exact moment to send the missile hurtling through the air.

To land in the dirt at the side of the lizard's skull.

Dumarest was running even as it left the pouch, lips drawn back, legs pounding, breathing in short, shallow gasps to oxygenate his lungs. To gain energy and speed so that, even as the half-stunned lizard headed toward cover he was on it, snatching up the prize, holding it fast as his teeth dug into the scaled throat and released the blood of its life.

Blood he gulped until it ceased to flow and then to fight the temptation to rip into the flesh and fill his stomach with its raw sweetness.

A boy forcing himself to think like a man.

A child of ten fighting to survive.

The place which was home rested ten miles distant over torn and hostile ground, the surface cut and scarred with crevasses edged with fused blades of obsidian, craters of starred silicates, mounds of bristling fragments blasted from the rubble of mountains. A journey which had to be taken with care for a slip could mean a broken leg and that would lead to inevitable death.

It was dark by the time he arrived and the fire was a warm beacon in the gloom. The only welcome he would get but, with luck, he would be given a portion of his kill. A hope which died as the man came to the mouth of the cave to snatch it and send him reeling with a vicious, back-handed blow.

"Lazy young swine! What took you so long?" He didn't wait for an answer, standing tall and puffed, his scarred face twisted into a snarl. "You've been eating!"

"It's on your mouth! Blood!"

"From the lizard! I—"

"Liar!" Again the thudding impact of the hand, a blow which smashed against his nose and sent his own blood to join the dried smears already on his chin. "You useless bastard! I took you in, let my woman tend you, and all you do is lie! A day's hunting for this!" He shook the dead reptile. "Well, it's too bad for you. Stay out there and starve!"

"I'll freeze!"

"So freeze. What's that to me? Freeze and be dammed to you!"

Another blow and he was gone, snug within the confines of the cave, warmed by the fire and fed by the game Dumarest had won. From where he crouched he could hear the mutter of voices, the harsh, cackling laughter of the crone as she heard the news, a liquid gurgling as the man lifted a mug from his pot of fermenting liquids.

Later there were snortings and muffled poundings and the sounds of animals in rut. Later still came snores.

From where he had crouched Dumarest rose and rubbed cracked palms over his frozen limbs. The incident had not been new; often he had been treated like that before, but then it had been summer and the nights had been warm and he had been fortunate. Now the neighbor who had fed him was dead and the rest had no time for charity.

If he stayed in the open he would die.

He knew it as he knew that he had been robbed of his kill and would continue to be robbed while the man had the greater strength. As always he would be robbed unless he prevented it. A hard-won lesson and one which would be wasted unless he survived to put it into practice. And he intended to survive.

Softly he stepped toward the cave and pushed aside the curtain of skins which closed the opening. The fire burned low, little more than a bed of glowing ashes but they radiated a welcome heat and he squatted beside them warming his hands and rubbing them over his legs and biceps. From the pot standing beside the embers he found a bone and sucked it, cracking it between his teeth to extract the marrow before throwing the shards on the fire where they burned with little blue flickerings of brightness.

More followed until the pot was empty and, drugged by

the nourishment, outraged muscles demanding rest, he fell asleep.

And woke to a scream of rage.

It was day and in the light seeping through the curtain the crone stood glaring at him, her raddled face convulsed with fury. A slut, her body sagging beneath the filthy clothes she wore, lice crawling in her matted hair, sores on lips and chin. A fit mate for the man who woke and lurched forward wiping the crust from his eyes.

"He's eaten it!" A cracked and dirty nail pointed at the pot. "The stew's gone! The thieving young bastard!"

"I'll teach him." The man pushed her aside. "I'll have the skin off his bones." He was naked aside from an apron around his loins. Stripping off the belt, he let it fall to reveal pallid, scabrous flesh. The leather whined as he swung it through the air. "Now you greedy young swine! Stand still and be taught a lesson!"

Stand and have the flesh scarred on back and thighs, bruised, cut with the edge of the belt, the heavy buckle weighting the end. Stand and be crippled, maimed, blinded. Stand and be killed!

Dumarest moved as the belt lashed toward him, feeling the stir of wind on his back through his torn garment. Unimpeded, the heavy buckle swung on to crack against the woman's arm. Her scream was echoed by the man's savage curse.

"Stand! Damn you, do as I say!"

He lunged forward, eyes blazing, face like that of an animal. The belt lifted, swung, again cut air as again Dumarest dodged. The third attempt was more successful and fire seared his shoulders. Trying to dodge the next blow he trod into the fire and the smouldering ashes seared his naked foot. Stumbling he fell to twist as leather lashed at his legs, his groin, one hand reaching out, feeling heat, fire which seared as he gripped a handful of embers and flung them into the snarling face.

"God!" The man screamed as he clawed at his face. "My eyes! My eyes!"

The woman was fast. Water showered from a pot and washed away the ashes to reveal eyes filled with streaming tears, bloodshot but otherwise unharmed. A face which was now a killer's mask.

"I'll get you," he panted. "I'll make you pay for that. By God I'll have you screaming before I've done with you."

Naked he advanced, belt forgotten, hands extended, the fingers curved into claws, instruments of destruction to grip and tear and savage the object of his hate.

A man against a child.

Dumarest backed and felt the touch of wind against his shoulders as he left the cave. It was barely dawn and a milky opalescence softened the harsh outlines of the terrain. Wisps of fading mist clung to the face of the cliff, shredding as the man lunged through writhing vapors, forming a curtain to create an isolated area of combat.

But how to fight a man five times heavier than himself?

Dumarest backed faster and felt his foot strike against a stone. Stooping, he snatched it up and held it so as to threaten.

"Stop! Leave me alone!"

"Begging, you little bastard?" The man gloated, enjoying the moment. "Well, beg on, boy. I owe you nothing. Nothing but the beating of your life!"

The stone could be thrown but if it missed what then? A second stone would provide a second weapon and Dumarest looked for one as he backed. To run would be safer but where could he go? And if he tried and slipped the man would be on him.

His sling?

It was bound around his waist and to loosen it would take too long. He needed a weapon to hand, one he could get to fast and use even faster. Another stone to back the first. A stone!

He found it as the man charged.

Dumarest rose and dived to one side all in the same flowing movement. Landing, he turned and, drawing back his arm, hurled one of his stones. His aim was good and the man roared as it hit his temple. Slapping his hand against the spot, he glared at the blood on his palm and, as he lowered it, Dumarest knew he intended to kill. Had intended it all along, perhaps, but now there could be no mistaking his intention.

How to win?

How to beat the mass of rage-inflamed muscle and bone? How to cripple it and bring it down and then make it harmless in the only way there was? Backing, stone in hand, Dumarest looked at the man as if he were a beast. He was a beast, a savage predator who must be stopped, one who would have no mercy.

The legs?

Smash his knees and he must fall. He would lie on the dirt unable to hurt anything beyond the range of his arms. He would twist and plead and cry in his pain and be an easy target for more missiles.

The genitals?

Better if they could be hit with enough force but the blow would have to be just right and the target wouldn't be easy to hit and was smaller than a knee. The rest of the body was hair and muscle and composed of tough sinew and bone.

The eyes?

Dumarest remembered the scream, the naked display of terror, the fear of blindness the man had revealed. The eyes, then. Vulnerable but an even smaller target than the groin and a lowering of the head could protect them. But that very action would serve to blind the man's vision and behind the eyes rested the skull, the brain, and below them the mouth and teeth and, lower, the throat.

And, already, he had hit a temple.

The second stone left his hand, flung with all the force of his back and shoulders, sliding through the air to hit the man's upraised arm, to fall to one side leaving nothing more than a bruise. A mistake, he should have used the sling, and he tore it from around his waist as the man lunged after him.

He was fast and Dumarest felt his hand touch his shoulder, slipping as fear gave him speed, the fingers catching the neck of his garment to jerk the rotting fabric from the thin, young body. A jerk which threw him off balance so that he stumbled and fell and cried out as the man fell on him, feeling the pound of a fist against his nose, the crushing of cartilage, the splitting of lips, the taste of blood in mouth and throat.

The feel of the soft bag as he desperately reached for the man's groin and gripped the testicles. The shriek as he jerked and twisted and pulled with nails dug deep, moving his head just in time to avoid the blow which broke bones as the man

rammed his hand against the rock, rolling clear to leave his
opponent moaning, grabbing at his loins, blood thick between
his thighs.

Time won in which to pick up stones and fit one to his
sling. To whirl it. To release the thong and watch as the missile smashed teeth. To send another, another, more until the
shrieking, blood-stained thing with the ruined eyes and pul-
verized face and the gray of brain showing among the red of
blood and white of bone finally slumped and was silent.

The woman said nothing as he entered the cave but silently
handed him a bowl of water, her eyes frightened, little suck-
ing noises coming from her lips. Her man was dead, who was
to provide? The boy was better than nothing. A decision
which kept her hand from the knife tucked into her rags but
Dumarest noticed the twitch of her hand and was cautious as
he washed blood from his nose and mouth.

The flesh was swollen and would soon show purple bruises
and be tender but as yet he could touch it without too much
discomfort. Snorting, he cleared his nostrils of clotted blood
and fumbled with the damaged organ. It looked lopsided but
that could have beeen distortion caused by the ruby-tinted
water which he used as a mirror.

"He hurt you." The woman was at his side judging the
time right to establish her authority. "He was drunk, mad,
crazed and dangerous. I was afraid of him. That's why I
couldn't help you last night."

And why she had screamed in rage this morning?

"I tried to stop him," she continued. "He pushed me aside.
You didn't see that, you were out of the cave by then. The
bastard hurt me." She winced as she pressed a hand to her
side. "He was always hurting me. I'm glad he's dead. You did
a good job out there. Gave him what he asked for. That nose
hurt?"

"No."

"It will." She lifted her hands toward him. "Unless you let
me fix it you'll have trouble later on. It'll block your breathing."

Dumarest said, "Give me your knife."

"Knife? Knife? What the hell are you talking about?"

"The knife," he said again. "The one in your skirt. I just

want to see it." Then, as she continued to shake her head, he added, "I might be able to make one like it. It'll be useful when hunting. I'll be able to get us more food."

"You'll hunt for me?" Dirt cracked in the creases of her face as she smiled. "You're a good boy, Earl. I've always thought of you as my own. Stick with me and I'll look after you. Stand by me and we'll get on fine."

"The knife." He held out his hand for it. "I'll look at it while you fix my nose."

It was crude, a strip of pointed and edged metal with slats of wood to form a grip, the whole held together with lashings of twine. He turned it as her fingers pressed at his nose, pushing the cartilage back into place, roughly shaping the damaged tissue. He was young and time would take care of the rest.

"There." She stepped back, dropping her hands. "You finished with my knife?"

"I'm keeping it."

"Keeping it?" Her voice rose in a shriek of protest. "Stealing it, you mean. First you kill my man then you rob me. Why stop there? Why not kill me too? Go ahead, you vicious young swine. Kill me. Kill me, I dare you!" Her face changed as he lifted the blade. "No! No, I didn't mean that!"

"How do you sharpen it?"

"What?"

"How do you sharpen it? With a stone or a file? If you have a file I want that too."

"A stone," she said bitterly. "I haven't a file. Not now. He sold it for a bottle. You might find another in the ruins." She watched as he moved about the cave. "What are you doing now? Robbing me some more?"

"I need clothes."

Clothes and food and something to carry it in. Water and a container for that too. A blanket against the cold of night and coverings for his feet to protect them against the stones. All the things which an adult had and which he had been denied because he was a child. But he was a child no longer. He had killed and was now a man.

And would leave and walk toward the east and live how he could.

Ten years old—a native of Earth.

The captain had an old, lined face with tufted eyebrows and a pinched nose set above a firm-lipped mouth. His skin was creped, mottled and pouched beneath the eyes. Thin hair graced a rounded skull. His hands toyed with a scrap of agate as they rested on his lap.

"Your name, boy?" He nodded as it was given. "Well, Earl, so you decided to stowaway. A mistake."

Dumarest said nothing.

"A bigger mistake than I think you realize. It is my duty to evict you into the void."

"To kill me, sir?"

"To punish you for having broken the regulations. You understand? Stowaways can't be encouraged, so to stop them we punish them when discovered. We didn't ask them to come aboard and they haven't paid for passage so we dump them as unwanted cargo." The eyes, deep-set beneath the tufted brows, watched him as the captain spoke. "You aren't afraid?"

"Of death, sir? Yes."

"Of course you are. Even the young fear death and you are how old? Ten? Eleven?"

"Yes, sir."

"Yes, what? Ten or eleven?"

"Eleven, sir—I think. Or I could be twelve."

"Aren't you sure?"

"No, sir." Dumarest looked at the man. "Does it matter?"

"Earth!" The captain made a spitting sound. "You poor little bastard!"

"Sir?"

"Forget it. I meant no insult. You've no family, of course? No kin. Nowhere to go and nothing to do when you' get there. What the hell could you lose by stowing away? How were you to know you were committing suicide?"

Dumarest made no comment, watching the movements of the hands as they toyed with the scrap of agate, the stone carved he saw now in the shape of a figure, a woman depicted with her knees updrawn to the chin, back and buttocks and thighs all blending in a continuous curve. The stone was worn with much handling.

"What am I to do with you?" muttered the captain. "Kill you, a boy? Toss you into the void because you acted from ignorance? Dump you like excreta into space? Were you born for such an end? Was anyone? Damn it, what to do?"

The stone slipped as he passed it from one hand to another, bounced on a knee and dropped to the deck. Dumarest caught it an inch before it landed.

"Sir!" He handed it to the man. Then saw the expression in the fading eyes, the lined face. "Sir?"

"Do you always move as fast as that?"

"It was falling and I didn't want it to get broken."

"So you lunged forward, stooped and caught it. Just like that." The captain tossed the carving into the air, caught it, tucked it into a pocket. "I've decided, lad. Are you willing to work hard? To learn? Damn it, I'll take a chance. You can work your passage. It's going to be a long trip and you'll work hard but, at least, you'll be fed."

Fed and rested and taught and one journey stretched to another and more after that until the captain had died and he'd moved on. Traveling deeper into the heart of the galaxy where stars were close and worlds plentiful. Into regions which had forgotten the world of his birth. Where the name of Earth was cause for amusement, the planet itself assumed to be a figment of legend.

"You understand why," said the captain. He had returned and was smiling. "No ships, nothing in the almanacs, no star guides, no coordinates. You're looking, Earl, but you are the only one convinced you have something to find."

"I'll find it."

"Yes." The man sobered. "Yes, Earl, you will. What else do you have to live for? But this," he gestured with a hand. "You know what all this is about?"

"I do."

"You'd better be sure of that."

"I am. I'm here to find Iduna."

"Yes," said the captain. "To find Iduna. So don't get yourself lost in the past. Childhood is over. And don't waste time in dreams—you have a job to do." His face wavered and began to blur. "You can call on me if ever you want someone to talk with."

"I know."

"Don't forget now. Don't forget."

And then he was gone.

Chapter Five

The wind was too strong creating turbulences which caught the raft and forced her to grip the rails to maintain her balance. From the thick mass of clouds lightning stabbed at the peaks, illuminating the mountains with bursts of savage radiance; electronic fire which gave the scene an unreal appearance as if it were a painting made by an insane artist. A harsh and brutal panorama yet one holding a raw beauty Kathryn could appreciate. For too long she had remained cooped behind walls. It was good to get out and feel the surge of elemental forces stirring her blood.

"My lady!" Shamarre lifted her voice above the wind. "We should drop. Drop!" She frowned as Kathryn shook her head.

The driver made the decision, dropping the raft and sending it heading away from the mountains and the dangerous air. An act she justified with a lifted hand pointing to a cluster of rafts high above.

Tamiras at work.

The vehicles were the largest available, cargo-carriers now filled with equipment and bales of prepared chemicals. Even as she watched they separated to climb high into the cloud, there to spray their loads of minute crystals which would trigger the reaction for the masses to release their water content in rain which would do little harm here over the mountains.

A hope and one he hadn't bolstered, shaking his head even as accepting the commission.

"We can try," he said bluntly, "All it will take is money for chemicals, but it could be money wasted. The formations are wrong. My other idea holds more promise."

To create energy fields in the atmosphere and use them as sweeps to push the clouds from sensitive areas. Brooms in the sky to brush away storms. If nothing else the man had audacity.

Kathryn glanced to where he had vanished in the clouds with his team. Men who followed him with a blind faith she could envy. Now they were willing to risk their lives because he led the way. Women would have been a little more cautious. They would have wanted safeguards and an assessment of the odds and would base their decisions on calculated probabilities. A trait which was regarded as admirable but which lacked a certain romance. Would she have been willing to ride into the nexus of a brewing storm knowing that, at any moment, naked fury could blast her into drifting atoms?

"My lady!" Shamarre was uneasy. Her broad face was lined with anxiety and her eyes were never at rest as they scanned earth and sky for signs of danger. Never comfortable in the air, she longed for dirt beneath her feet. "The storm—"

"Will break when it breaks and if Tamiras is lucky will do no harm."

"To the crops, no. But to us?"

Rain wouldn't hurt them though some had been drowned in storms, but hail could pound them to a jelly and the lightning could sear them with the fury of lasers. Yet still she hesitated to order the return. If mere men could brave the elements how could she do less?

And, out here, could be found a little, relative peace of mind.

"Look!" The driver lifted her arm. "The raft—look!"

It dropped from the clouds, turning, bales falling from the open body, bundles which jerked to a halt at the end of ropes as other shapes, also lashed, swung and grappled with the swinging loads. One of the fleet which had run into trouble, caught by opposing blasts, the driver taken by surprise or unable to maintain control. But he was skilled. Even as she watched, Kathryn saw the vehicle veer and swing, the crew shortening the ropes and heaving bales back where they belonged, the movements of the raft aiding their efforts.

From the carrier fell a shower of glinting crystals as one of the bales split open. A fall which spread in the wind to stream a swirl toward and above her. And, suddenly, the immediate area was drenched with rain.

It pounded on the raft, the housing, the people it contained, adding a fresh glisten to metal accoutrements and plastic fabrics. Rain which wet her face and hair and ran down her neck to send moisture seeping over her torso.

"He was wrong!" Shamarre was yelling her pleasure at this proof of the fallibility of men. "Tamiras was wrong!"

Seeding could make the clouds shed their water; the accident had proved it—or had it been a coincidence? And even if it had not it could have been a matter of luck. The more massive formations could be of a different "ripeness" and resistant to the primitive method which had seemed to work. Yet the man would try. No matter what, he would try.

Men, she thought. Weak, romantic fools for the most part. Illogical and immature even when nearing the end of their natural span. Who else would risk seemingly inevitable madness for the sake of an ideal? After the first few volunteers no other women had offered to go in search of Iduna. But men? Always there had been a man who, for some mysterious reason of his own, had agreed to take the chance. Was it their fault they had proved to be weak? If weakness had anything to do with it. What had Dumarest said?

She frowned, trying to remember and wondering why she couldn't. All connected with Iduna was crystal clear—her smile, the way she used to lift her hands, the pressure of her lips against her cheek when, without fail, she had gone to bid her good night. And, more than anything else, that dreadful moment she had seen her lying, apparently dead, the cursed bulk of the Tau lying beside her.

Iduna, her only child, why did slave women breed like vermin when she had been so denied?

"My lady, your pleasure?" The gust of rain had ceased and Shamarre, wet and chilled, wanted to get back to the palace. "You need a hot bath and change of clothing."

A hint as to what she herself longed for but she could wait. Perversity kept Kathryn from giving the order to return. Glancing up and back at the sky above the mountains she saw the dancing interplay of lightning; blasts which tore stone and sent rolling thunder to echo like a monstrous voice through shrouded valleys and jagged passes.

Surely the seeding must have been completed by now?

A vaggary of wind and the raft tilted a little to steady as the driver adjusted the controls, rising a little to meet another gust, to veer again, to spin beneath the impact of a sudden shower of hail.

"The storm!" Her voice rose in sudden terror. "The storm—it's breaking!"

Wind caught the raft as savage lightning ripped through clouds now venting showers of hail. Ice drummed on the metal and piled in heaps within the body of the vehicle, striking like hammers, stinging as if each pellet were a vicious insect. Head crouched, Kathryn felt Shamarre come to her, a thick cloak thrown as a shield over them both, the fabric supported by brawny arms.

Over the roar of the storm Kathryn shouted, "The driver! Tell her—"

"She has her orders." Shamarre was brusque. "And she isn't such a fool as to linger where there is danger just for the fun of it."

A reproof? Kathryn felt the shift of the raft as it headed back and down away from the storm and shifted beneath the cloak to maintain her balance. Shamarre, at times was outspoken but she had earned the right by long years of dedicated service and, anyway, the moment was too pleasurable to spoil by her taking umbrage at what could have been an emotive slip of the tongue.

Impatiently Kathryn pushed aside the cloak and looked back toward the mountains, seeing the dance of lightning, the mist of swirling rain, the sheets of ice which dropped to plaster the rocks with a crust of white. Hammers which no longer threatened the crops. Tamiras had won—but other problems remained.

The church was a flimsy construction of plastic spread over poles, mottled, stained, divorced of all pretension and aspirations of beauty; a strictly functional construct which occupied most of the space granted by the Matriarch and provided living quarters for the monks, a dispensary, a space in which a few could sit and rest while meditating or receiving instruction, a smaller space where a supplicant could find ease.

A cubicle in which Brother Remick sat behind the benediction light and watched the woman kneeling before him.

Once she had been young and still held a measure of attraction but now her face in the glowing, ever-shifting light from the instrument was taut, ugly with self-contempt as she babbled a list of minor sins. As she paused, the monk said quietly, "Is there nothing more, sister?"

"Nothing! I—"

"Can find contentment only in confession, my child. Admit

to yourself the wrong you have done to others and accept the punishment which will give ease and peace of mind. Guilt is corrosive and will eat into your mental and physical well-being. Rid yourself of it. Give voice to it. Nothing you say here before me will be repeated. It will be as if you spoke to yourself alone."

But by voicing the guilt she would ease it and, hypnotized by the swirling colors of the benediction light, she would respond to his suggestions and suffer a subjective penance before being wakened and given the scrap of concentrates which form the bread of forgiveness. Many came for that alone, confessing minor sins and accepting the mild penances for the sake of the food. A fair exchange—once under the influence of the light each was indoctrinated with the command never to kill.

Others followed, at times it seemed as if the suppliants were endless, but finally the monk was able to rise from his chair and ease the ache of bone and muscle. Outside the air held a peculiar dampness and the late afternoon sun was tinged with swirls of lambent emerald which traced deeper patterns of green against the sky. The residue of the distant storm which was either dying or moving deeper into the mountains. In the slanting light the town was a trap for shadows, patches of relative gloom accentuating the high-flung grace of tower and spire and pinnacle. The triple arches of the palace soared like challenging fingers against the bowl of the firmament.

Beauty—why did it have to be sullied?

A question the monk had asked often before and had yet to gain a satisfying answer.

Worlds circled their suns like jewels caught in the web of space and each held its own, unique charm. Yet each, once touched by man, grew the vicious cancers of greed and hate and domination. Forests destroyed for the cellulose they contained, the ground ravaged for minerals, the seas spoiled for fish, the land for game. Man was a blight, a disease, a thing of terror. An animal which had learned to think and build but which had never developed the capacity for compassion.

"Brother?" Echo was at his side, the old monk's face masked by his cowl. "If I intrude—"

"You do not. Juba?"

The monk was within the living quarters, lying supine on

his narrow cot, his eyes closed in a waxen face, his thin hands resting on his stomach. For a moment Remick stood looking down at him, noting the sunken cheeks, the darkly circled eyes, the flaccidity of the skin at jaw and throat. Touching the wrist he felt a barely discernible pulse. The skin itself was febrile.

"How long?"

"An hour after you took your station, Brother. I thought he was sleeping and did what I could before attending the dispensary. A short while ago I checked and found him as you see." The calmness of his voice faltered a little. "Is there hope?"

There was always hope—but not for Brother Juba. He was dying and they both knew it. Soon now he would be dead and a life of absolute dedication would be over. And what was there to show for it? What mark would he have left? The sacrifice of personal comforts, of a wife and children, of the chance of wealth and the relinquishing of all self-pride and all self-determination—what had it achieved? Worlds still were ruled by terror, men and women were still slaves, hatred and cruelty still held domination. Men still looked on each other as things less than human. There was still pain.

And, always, there would be death.

A part of the Natural Cycle which ruled all things. To be born, to grow and then to die. The old making way for the young and the young growing to build for those who would come after. And all passing into the Great Unknown and all, at the end, truly equal.

As Echo left the cramped quarters Remick settled down to his vigil. Perhaps he should have let the other do it, the monks had been close, but it was his duty and it would have been no kindness to force the other to witness a preview of his own end. Soon he too would be making the last journey and then would be time enough for him to be involved with thoughts of extinction. Now the living, those waiting for medical aid, would occupy his mind and turn his thoughts from the still figure on the cot.

Again Remick touched the hand, his fingers searching automatically for the pulse. Drugs could restore the flush to the sunken cheeks but it would be a temporary illusion and only a momentary staving off of the inevitable end. And a man should be allowed to die in dignity, not hooked and incorporated into a machine, a part of devices which pumped blood and air and adjusted the endocrine balance and turned the body of man into a thing of mechanics.

A respite gained at what cost?

Remick had seen such things in the big hospitals on wealthier worlds and had seen, too often, the fear and greed and envy such things induced. To live! To last another day, another hour! To stave off death. To linger no matter what the cost. To squander the accumulated wealth of years and rob the young of their patronage. To glory in the cult of self. To yearn for immortality.

Madness!

Death was a part of life. An ending. A closing. Something to be accepted with calmness and equanimity. The end of an episode and the beginning of another. Birth, growth, death—the sum total of life and of existence.

"Brother!" On the cot Juba stirred, tongue touched dried lips. As Remick fed him water his voice strengthened a little yet still remained detached. "Don't leave me, Brother. How am I to manage? I know so little and must accomplish so much. Brother!"

An appeal to some long-dead monk who had been his guide and mentor when young. Remick knew the feeling well, the awesome sense of responsibility when, filled with zeal, he had set out to change the universe. An ambition all monks shared and one which slowly lost its luster as the realization was accepted that one man could do only so much and to change human nature was to attempt the near impossible.

"No!" Juba turned, twisting, sweat dewing his face and neck. "No! For the love of God, don't! Don't!"

A revived fragment of memory surfacing like a bubble on a pond, to burst and release agony. To make the past real and immediate again, a time when, still young, Juba had been taken by regressed primitives and subjected to their torture of fire. Beneath his robe his body showed the scars; savage wounds reaching to his waist, burned areas mottled in purple and angry red. They could be clearly displayed, but the other scars, those on his mind, had been buried deep.

Now to rise and produce screams and writhings then a panting submission as Remick touched major nerves and spoke soothing words to diminish the impact with hypnotic skill.

A kindness and the reason why no monk was ever allowed to die alone if it was possible to attend him. A reassurance that he was not alone, that he would never be alone, that always there would be someone who cared. The final seal of a fellowship which embraced them all in a common cause.

"Brother!" Remick closed his fingers on those in his hand. "Rest easy, Brother, all will be well. Peace will be yours. Now rest and dream of scented fields on which shines the warm light of a brilliant sun. See how the flowers stir to the breeze and how the butterflies lift to soar and wheel in flashes of glowing color. Rest, Brother. Rest."

Juba sighed but the weight on his mind was too great to be so easily banished. When he next spoke his voice was that of a child, thin, detached, impersonal. Remick listened, his face intent, unsurprised at what he heard. Men were not angels and no man, not even a monk, could live a life free of sin. Always were temptations of the flesh, of ambition, of anger and irritation. The sin of pride was always close as were the sins of arrogance and impatience. Of rage and hate and intolerance. Things absolved by confession and subjective penance to be committed again perhaps, but the monks were men not robots, to err was human.

And Juba had lived a long time.

It was dark when Remick left the shack and stepped into the open. Far in the distance lightning still flickered over the mountains but the air was clearer now and stars could be seen glittering in the dark bowl of the sky. At the gate men clustered, talking, casual as they guarded the field and the field itself was almost deserted. A trader from Logaris and a vessel on its way to Klandah. A man was working on its lowered ramp.

Life and vessels which spanned the void, work and idle talk and, even as he took a deep breath of the air, the sudden spurt of laughter.

And, behind him, death.

Echo came toward him, eyes questioning in the lines of his face, the face itself framed by his thrown-back cowl.

"Juba?"

"Is gone. He died in peace." Remick rested his hand on the other's shoulder. "You knew him well?"

"Almost from the beginning. We learned in the same seminary and undertook our first mission together. On Flagre. I

fell sick there and almost died. He saved me but I had to return to Pace for extensive treatment. I heard from him from
time to time after that but it wasn't until now we worked together." Pausing Echo said, "A good man. I shall miss him."

"We shall all miss him." Remick again drew air deep into
his lungs. "Now I must inform the Matriarch of his passing."

Tamiras said, "Dead? A monk dead? How droll." Wine
swirled in the goblet he supported with slender fingers. "But
why tell you? Surely the Matriarch of Esslin has better things
to occupy her attention?"

Before Kathryn could answer, Gustav said, "A matter of
courtesy, I imagine. The church is here by sufferance and
must know it."

"And could want more land? More privileges?" Tamiras
reached for a bowl of nuts and, holding a pair in one hand,
cracked them by a sudden pressure. "Don't make the mistake
of underestimating the monks. There had been a scuffle,
right? The old man had got hurt in some way. Now he is
dead and it could be thought that you might feel guilty."

"Guilty?"

"Responsible then." Tamiras shrugged. "The men who did
the hurt were your guards. You might feel moved to grant a
further tract of land or give financial support or something
like that in recompense." He ended dryly, "Little do they
know the ruler of this happy world."

Sarcasm, the man was full of it. Watching him, Kathryn
noted the deeply lined face, the thin, pursed lips, the straggle
of hair he affected around lips and chin. A beard which
verged on the grotesque and added to his monkey-like appearance. An aging man trying to emulate youth with his
gaudy finery, his jewels, his laces and pomades, the curled
hair which ringed his high, balding brow. But not a fool.

A vicious, spitefully stinging wasp perhaps, but never a
fool.

Gustav said slowly, "You could be wrong, Tamiras.
Brother Remick didn't strike me as being a greedy man. He
made no demands."

"And so proved his cleverness."

"How?"

"By leaving the matter in question. A demand could meet
with acceptance or refusal—either way the matter is ended.

As it is you are left with doubt. Should you be generous or not? If not then you feel a touch of guilt and—"

"Guilt!" Kathryn's goblet slammed hard on the table. "You use the word too often for my liking, Tamiras. Why should I feel guilty?"

"What we do we pay for. Sooner or later we pay."

Was the man insane? Staring at him Kathryn began to regret the impulse which had made her invite him to dinner. He had done well, true, but his prickly qualities alienated any true regard. And his innuendoes were becoming irksome. Now, it seemed, he was talking in riddles.

Gustav said sharply, "We pay, Tamiras. One way or another we pay. How true. With tears, perhaps. With lost opportunities. Even with pain. That received from impalement, for example."

"A statutory lesson." Tamiras picked at his crushed nuts, fingers selecting fragments of kernel, lips moving busily as he thrust them into his mouth. "But what does it teach? The warning to obey is wasted on a man who is never given the chance to rebel."

"But not on those watching." Kathryn lifted her goblet to be refilled by the servant standing behind her chair. "They remember."

"Who? The nobles? The rick ladies who have time to enjoy the fun? What do they need with such lessons? The workers, perhaps? Those too busy to stand and wait and make bets on how long the victim will last? The slaves?" He picked at his nuts not looking at her. "A pity," he mused. "I used too much force. The husk was driven into the meat."

With a sudden blaze of anger she understood.

Not his concern over the punishment but his manner of letting her know how useless he thought it to be. And the rest? The earlier talk of guilt? She remembered his mother back in the early days of her rule. The woman had joined a cabal and fled when the rebellion had been thwarted. Together they had lived in exile and Tamiras had only returned to Esslin after her death. Would he still bear a grudge?

He had been old then, fully grown and studying on an industrial world. A whim of his mother's, but Vaada had been a stupidly ambitious woman. And had there been a marriage of some kind? An alliance with a low-born family? She must remember to ask Gustav about it.

Now she said, "We are bound by custom, Tamiras, as you well know. Impalement is legal execution for certain crimes. And why feel sorry for those who deserve it? Did anyone force them to break the law?"

"In certain circumstances that could be the case."

"Explain!"

"A slave is property," he said carefully. "He or she must obey the owner. Now, suppose that owner were to order the slave to commit a crime—who would be to blame?"

"The owner."

"And who would testify against him? Who but the slave." He smiled as she remained silent. "You see how it could be?"

"We have procedures for such cases."

"The irons? The rack? The tools with which our ancestors wrung the truth from stubborn lips? But who was put to the questions? The slaves, naturally, for it was obvious they must be lying."

"And what is your suggestion for eliminating this abuse of power if any such abuse exists?" Gustav leaned forward from where he sat. "Your polygraphs?"

"What else?" Tamiras became alive now that his subject had been touched on, his eyes gaining a brighter fire. "Lie-detectors for all. An accusation is made, the one making it is tested as to veracity, those denying the charge also probed. A fast and efficient method of arriving at the truth and one used on a multitude of worlds. No judge, no jury, no defense counsels. Just a machine and an arbitrator."

"Souless perfection," said Kathryn. "It would never be permitted on Esslin."

"Because too many women wish to cling to their positions of power. To sit in judgment and claim infallibility. What else to expect in a culture which tolerates slavery?" Shrugging, he added, "I'll give the monks their due on that. They hate it."

"Slavery?" Kathryn changed the subject. "What do they really believe in? Not just their credo but the rest. Why do they suffer so much privation without real need?"

"As an example." Tamiras looked at the wine in his goblet and now his tone was free of mocking inflections. "They help the poor and are poor as anyone can see. No fine clothing, no jewels, no luxurious quarters. No monk is ever better dressed or better fed than his followers. This is true on all worlds I have visited."

"They love poverty?"

"They hate it. To them it is a disease. They fight it in every way they can. There is no virtue in suffering. There is no grace to be found in pain. But as for what they believe, well—"

"They believe that all living things are the parts of a whole," said Gustav quietly. "That the intelligences which reside in the multiplicity of brains are akin to the individual cells of a body. All is one and one is all. Death is a rejoining of the individually aware scrap of consciousness with the great, common pool. You, I, all of us are as the fingers of a hand. We do not know we are simply the extensions of a far more complex being. If you choose to call that common pool God, then you are as correct as any other."

"You know about these things?" Tamiras sounded astonished. "Gustav, you amaze me!"

"Because I have read and studied and arrived at certain conclusions? You, a student of science, to find that strange?"

"Hardly a student," said Tamiras dryly. "My school days are far behind me and yet I will admit there is always something new to learn. The behavior of the storm, for example. I would have sworn that seeding the clouds was a waste of time and yet, somehow, we succeeded. Why? A shift in the electromagnetic potential of the area? A minute alteration in water content? Something which affected the ionization of the clouds? Who can tell?"

"Can't you find out?" The information could be important and urgency edged her voice as Kathryn fired the question. "Surely your instruments would have yielded the information?"

"Instruments?" His ironic smile made her remember the raft she had seen, the men swinging from their ropes, "What instruments? We carried chemicals and little else. We were lucky, that's all."

"So you don't think that similar precautions would work again? Or rather you cannot guarantee they would?" Gustav pursed his lips as Tamiras shook his head. "So it comes back to your fields. But how are you going to brace them against the thrust of moving masses of air?"

"It is all in my report. Towers must be set at regular intervals along the line of the foothills. They must be strongly braced and equipped with balancing fields in order to lock the entire installation into the planetary crust." China rattled as Tamiras, suddenly vibrant, pushed aside the table furnishing in order to clear a space. "See?" He set items on the cloth; knives, spoons, trails of salt, patches of spice. "Lock a field here and another here and we have a buttress which will withstand any storm threatening this area. Power could be supplied from installations built here and here with double compensators and automatic feedback relays." His finger rapped at the table. "By cross-linking we shall be able to utilize all generated energy at any one point as needed. Once built the installations will protect the crops against snow and hail and anything the mountains can develop. Yields will increase and we could even gain an extra planting a year."

"But at a price." Gustav mused over the rough plans. "What if portable installations could be built? Massed rafts to bear the heavy equipment which could be sent out as the need became manifest? Power could also be supplied from mobile sources and would only be used to give protection when actually needed. At other times they could serve factories and remote areas. You see my point? It would be less expensive and more versatile."

"But less efficient."

"Only relatively so. If . . ."

Kathryn leaned back in her chair as the discussion continued. Her head ached a little and it was a relief to close her eyes but darkness brought no consolation. Against her lids she could see the pale beauty of Iduna, the Tau, the face of Dumarest now lying in an apparent coma.

Heard again the voice of the technician who attended him.

"No response as yet, my lady, but that is all to the good. As far as we can determine his normal processes are unimpaired." Then she'd added, spoiling it all, "Of course it's early to tell yet. For all we know his mind could have gone as did the others."

Damn the stupid bitch! Couldn't she at least have left her with hope? If Dumarest failed what else did she have?

Chapter Six

He sat on a rock in a plain of coarse, volcanic sand, black grains which stretched as far as he could see to a horizon limned with smouldering ruby. Flame which rose to cover the sky with swirling tendrils of somber red and darting, orange, strands and swaths of savage color edged with black, the black fading to scarlet, to crimson, to fill his eyes with the hue of blood.

A sky Dumarest had never seen before, a plain which was strange.

He moved, feeling the solidity of the stone beneath him, the grate of sand against his boots. He was dressed now, the knife snug in its sheath, warm and divorced from the need of food and water. Able to think and plan and review the situation.

He had run to the Tau as a child. As Iduna must have run to it to hold it close in infantile delight at a strange novelty. Luminosity had engulfed him and, suddenly, he had been elsewhere. In a nursery furnished as if for a giant fitted with walking, talking toys. But a child saw things in a different perspective and would think of normal furniture as being large. The dolls too—many a child had dolls as large as itself. Iduna had been spoiled and would have had such toys.

He had passed into a place fitted for the girl, one which to her would have been familiar, and then he had left it to re-live again his own childhood. A portion of it—had there been more? Dumarest frowned, thinking, trying to remember. Had there been another woman who would have been kind to him? A man? He couldn't remember. Even the faces of the others who must have lived close in the settlement were nothing but blurs. Only the man had seemed real. The man he had killed and the woman he had left after taking her knife. And then?

79

The ship and the captain and, suddenly, this plain.

An area which could hold unexpected dangers. The volcanic sand would be loose and easy to shift and serve to provide burrows for lurking predators. The sky itself seemed to be flaring warnings and Dumarest felt his nerves tense with the old, familiar signal of impending danger. A tension which increased as he heard the faint rasp of shifting grains.

Sand moving when there was no wind!

He lunged forward, rising, his hand dropping, lifting with the weight of the knife as he turned to face horror.

It was big, looming against the sky, a thing of spined limbs and oozing palps, of mandilbles which snapped with the rattle of castanets, of eyes which glowed like jewels mounted in short, bristling hair. An insect, armored and armed with glistening plates of chitin, multi-eyed, multi-limbed. A thing three times the size of a man which reared from the sand in a rain of black granules to scuttle toward its prey.

Dumarest sprang to one side and felt his boot slip in the sand so that, thrown off balance, he swung beneath the sweep of a claw to fall, to roll desperately as serrated edges tore at the sand to leave long, ugly furrows. A moment in which the thing heaved itself totally from the black grains to rear in monstrous silhouette against the flame-shot sky, to turn as it fell, to land and lunge forward in one flickering movement.

Dumarest rose, diving to one side, blade lifted to ward off the slash of a spined limb, steel biting into chitin to release a gush of yellow ichor, to thrust at the membrane of a joint, to dig and twist and leave the thing with a crippled limb.

A minor wound which it ignored as, poised, it stood watching.

A thing which lurked beneath the sand, waiting for unguessable hours for prey to alert it to the possibility of food and moisture. Stimulated by his scent, the meat he carried, the fluid his skin contained.

And against it Dumarest had nothing but his knife.

It wasn't enough and he'd known it from the first. The creature was too big, the blade too short to penetrate to a vital organ. The eyes he could attack but they were many and even if totally blinded the thing could trace him by scent. The limbs could be crippled but, again, there were too many. To destroy them all would be to leave it a helpless mass writhing in the sand but to do it would require speed and skill as well as judgment and luck. Too much luck.

But he had to try.

Stooping he snatched up sand in his left hand and darted forward as he threw it at the eyes of the creature. Even as the grains left his hand he lunged to the attack, knife a shimmer as he struck, slashed, twisted at joints and softer portions. A moment in which he seemed to be winning then again the thing reared, revealing an underside blotched and mottled with tufted hairs, legs scrabbling as it twisted, falling to smash against him, one leg numbing his arm with a blow which tore the knife from his fingers and sent it spinning to clash against the rock.

As the limb returned for another blow Dumarest caught it in both hands, threw his weight against it, strained until chitin yielded and the broken appendage flopped in streams of sickly yellow. A minor victory and possibly his last. Stars exploded in his skull as a living club slammed against his head and the twitch of the broken limb he held flung him up and away to land heavily in the sand.

To lie and die.

To rise and run and die.

To overcome his weakness, the dizziness, the stench of the insect, to return to the battle, to do what he could against impossible odds and, because they were impossible, to die.

Always it came to that.

Bare-handed he was helpless and even if he still had the knife the end would have been the same. He needed a laser, a heavy-duty weapon which would burn holes in the thing like a red hot wire in butter. A military-type Mark IV Ellman such as he had used before.

And, suddenly, he had it.

Dumarest rose as the thing charged, the gun cradled in his arms, finger closing on the release as a serrated claw moved to cut him in half. A claw which smoked and jerked and turned on the end of its limb to fall in a shower of yellow as the red guide-beam traced a searing path over the natural armor. A ruby finger which lifted to turn jeweled eyes into patches of char. To send destruction in a swath between the gaping mandibles. To fry the soft inner tissues. To reach the main ganglion and caress it and turn it into ash with the heat of its passion.

To kill!

Dumarest lowered the gun as the creature fell, feeling the weight of it in his hands as thin limbs scrabbled at the sand, the creature threshing in reflex action, black grains rising to fall with whispering rustles. Rustles which were repeated on all sides. Mounting into a hideous chittering as the plain boiled with ferocious life.

The dead thing had not been alone.

Dumarest flung himself against the rock as they came scuttling toward him. A mass of insect-like things grotesquely huge, some like mutated spiders, others with the claws and stings of scorpions, more like racing ants, all objects of potential death.

Some met the ruby guide-beam of the laser and fell to be torn apart by others. Others, crippled, lurched away, fighting off those who would feed on their still-living flesh. The rest, uninjured, advanced like running horses over the sand. An endless stream of them which covered the area with shifting patterns of red and scarlet; the sky reflected in the sea of glistening chitin.

Against them the gun was useless.

Dumarest turned, fired, turned and fired again, turned and fired in a circle which ringed him with a mound of dead and smouldering flesh but still they came on filling the air with the rasp of their passage; the harsh clatter of mandibles the chittering of joints and antennae and lifted stings, the scrape of hooked and reaching feet.

One laser—he needed an army!

And, suddenly, he had it.

Men were all around him, grim figures in battle armor, tough mercenaries wearing familiar colors. They dropped into position and built a barrier of crossfire in which nothing living could survive. Darting flashes of laser beams weaving a tapestry of brilliance against the sky. A web of destructive energies directed with the skill of long training. Against such a barrage men would have retreated but the creatures on the plain were not men. With insensate ferocity they continued the attack.

And the red of human blood joined the yellow of spilled ichor.

A man screamed as a claw closed around his waist, lifting him high, closing to let him fall in two parts joined by a shower of crimson. Another tried to run and fell with twitching stumps where legs had been. A third, his face ripped from the bones of his skull, staggered, keening, hands lifted to the ghastly mask until a comrade gave him the mercy of a quick end.

Incidents which stood out among the rest but on all sides men cried out and fell and died beneath the weight of the ceaseless onslaught. Firing, Dumarest climbed on the rock, eyes narrowed as he scanned the distances, seeing yet more creatures and, among them, man-like shapes.

Figures which stood, watching, hands thrust into the wide sleeves of their robes. Robes which glowed scarlet beneath the sky. Cowls which hide the faces but, if the faces were hidden, the device marked in the breast of each robe was not.

The Cyclan—here?

Enigmatic figures which served as targets for the weapon Dumarest lifted to aim and fire. Shapes which wilted only to reappear elsewhere. And, all around, the noise and fury of combat.

Screams and chitterings and the hiss of ichor turned into steam. The near-inaudible hissing of laser fire turning air-borne moisture into vapor. The grunts of men recognizing inevitability. The curses which accompanied the fore-knowledge of death.

"Keep firing!" Dumarest shouted from his position on the rock. "Maintain positions and coordinate your action. Drop and shoot upward. Keep them back."

Back until, surely, there could be no more. Back until the air grew hot and the plain steamed with noxious vapors. Until guns ceased to fire as stored energies failed. Back until men died and lay where they had fallen with tormented faces turned to an alien sky. Until Dumarest, thrown to one side, knowing he was hit, realized he was dying.

His tunic had been ripped open and the chest beneath was a mass of blood and torn muscle, pulped tissue flecked with the white shards of shattered ribs. Breathing, he felt the rush of blood into laboring lungs and tasted its flavor. Trying to move, he sensed the shattered legs and felt agony jar his spine.

Still he tried to use the gun but now it was too heavy to lift. And his knife was gone. And the sky was darkening.

And he was small and alone and wanting, so desperately wanting, to be helped.

The miracle came in a bubble.

Dumarest watched as it came from over the horizon, a shimmering ball of rainbow colors to drift toward him, to settle and turn into a chamber fitted with a mass of medical equipment staffed by solemn-faced attendants. The plain too had changed; now it was an expanse of rolling sward dotted with brilliant flowers and the sky held the hues of spring, soft greens and delicate yellows tinged with cool violet and warming orange.

And he felt no pain.

Not when, suddenly, he was lying on the gleaming surface of a table with a golden-haired woman leaning over him, her face filled with admiration. Not when, somehow, she healed his wounds and he sat up, his clothing undamaged, the knife back in his boot.

And, as there had been no pain, now there were no corpses either of men or the things which had attacked him.

A thought and they had gone.

But the girl?

Dumarest looked at her as she stood as if waiting for him to speak. Tall, golden haired, her face round and impassive. A nurse or a physician—certainly she had healed him. Or at least he had been healed at the touch of her hands. Hands which, seemingly, had also repaired his clothing and replaced his knife.

Iduna?

She blinked as he asked and looked her astonishment.

"My lord I am Tarunda. To have served you is a pleasure I shall treasure for always."

Her voice was like the caress of a breeze on scented roses and her perfume sent fires running in his blood. A woman and one vaguely familiar. Where had he seen her before?

And why had he been attacked by giant insects?

They had come from the sand, boiling from the plain, too many to find food in such a place and too ferocious for things so large. They had come as if in a dream, a nightmare, and even when dead and dying they had held a sickening horror.

But he had met such forms before and had no fear of dif-

ferent forms of life. Sand and a red sky and creatures which
had attacked without warning and, vaguely seen in the background, the watching figures of cybers.

They at least he could understand, the tall shapes dressed
in scarlet represented a danger which had threatened him for
too long now. They and the organization they served, the
wide-flung and powerful Cyclan which manipulated men as if
they were puppets.

But here?

The girl worried him with her vague familiarity and he
stared at her trying to fit a place and background to the face
and figure. The hospital on Shallah? No, he had not seen her
there. In a tavern somewhere? There had been too many.
Tarunda? He mentally spoke the name. Tarunda of . . . of
. . . Tarunda!

And it was there before him.

The ring with the circle of watching faces, the smell, the
avid gleam of watching eyes. The animal-stink of fear and oil
and blood. The reek of anticipated pain. The knife gripped in
his sweating palm, ten inches of honed and polished steel, a
match to the one held by the man facing him. A tall, smiling,
feral shape with the blotch of a tattoo smeared across his
torso.

The shriek of a woman's voice.

"Get him, Spider! Slice him open and let's see the color of
his guts!"

His first commercial fight.

Dumarest could feel the impact of the floor beneath his
naked feet as he waited for the bell. Feel too the hunger
gnawing at his stomach. Fight and be fed. Win and get a
stake. Lose and what the hell has gone?

A young man, little more than a boy, still mourning the
death of his only friend, now forced to fight in order to
survive.

"Kill him!" screamed the woman again. "Kill him, Spider—and tonight you can crawl right into me!"

An invitation which sent slanted eyes flickering in her
direction as the bell jarred its harsh note. A moment in which
Dumarest acted, moving to the attack, cutting, drawing
blood, backing—to feel the burn and rip as steel laced a ruby
path over his ribs.

A mistake. He should have thrust and aimed for a vital

point or, no, he should have cut and cut again and not given the man time to get in a blow of his own. But how to gain the experience of years in a few brief minutes? How to match such acquired skill?

How to live long enough to learn?

Dumarest dodged as the man attacked, steel flashing, seeming to vanish, to reappear again in an unexpected place. Speed alone saved him, the thin, vicious whip of slashed air casting a transient breeze against his side. A blow which if it had landed would have cut him deep to show his insides..

A momentary display of anger on his opponent's part. Confident in his skill, he wanted to extend the bout so as to gain a cheap reputation. The wound he had taken was a minor cut, blood making it seem worse than it was, and it would be better to give the crowd a spectacle rather than a quick kill. The savage cut was a mistake he would not repeat.

Instead he would dart in to cut sinew and nerve and tendon, to leave Dumarest maimed and crippled and a mass of shallow, gaping wounds. An eye ruined, perhaps, an ear removed, the nose converted into gaping orifices, the lips slashed.

The young bastard would pay for getting in first!

He weaved, lunged, blinked as his edge missed flesh, felt the burn of another wound, the wet warmth of flowing blood. Dumarest, backing, watched the interplay of muscle on his opponent's thighs and calves. The set of the feet which signaled an attack, the lift of the hand to position the knife, the flash which he confidently parried—to feel the shock, the pain, the sear of slicing metal as another bloody adornment was cut into his torso.

A cut which could have been a thrust which could have found his heart. Blood which flowed from his ribs but which even now could be spurting from his stomach. A mistake the man had made. He should have gone in for the kill while he had the chance. Now, grimly determined, Dumarest realized that to survive he must kill.

Steel clashed, parted, blades meeting again to emit thin, high ringing notes which hung in the fevered air like the distant chiming of bells. Dumarest dodged, felt the burn of another wound, cut back in turn and dodged again as the more experienced man continued his attack with a sweeping backhanded cut which changed to an upthrusting lunge. A master of his trade, one who had killed so often he had forgotten the count, one who now decided the fight had lasted long enough.

One whose confidence dug him a grave.

Dumarest was young and obviously a novice. He could be deluded and be made to appear a fool. For a moment only he would appear to have the advantage and then he would become meat for butchery. A screaming, whimpering, blood-ied thing which would lie on the canvas and stain it with his blood.

Then the blades touched again and the target which should have been within reach had vanished to dart in, to sting with naked steel, to back and dodge and run and hit again, and again, and again until the tattoo was lost beneath red and all thoughts lost but the need to get in and strike. To hit and kill!

A moment in which the watchers saw oiled bodies seeming to embrace, the glitter of blades, the pant, the meaty impact, the sudden spurting of crimson as, slowly, one fell to leave Dumarest standing, knife in hand, his torso a mess of blood.

And then Tarunda who had taken him to her home.

A harlot, she had been touched by his youth and igno-rance. A haunter of taverns who chased the flattering gloom of fire and candlelight and who, yielding to a whim, had nursed him back to health. Sewing his cuts and supplying an-tibiotics when they had festered and food to restore his ener-gies and, later, that which had made him one of many.

Tarunda—how had he forgotten her?

The years held the answer. Too many years and too many journeys and too many fights and too many other women who had wanted to help him and who had loved him in their fashion. But had she really looked as this girl looked now?

Dumarest studied her as she stood beside him patiently waiting. Young, lovely, the hair a mane of natural gold, the skin beneath the chin firm, the mouth lacking the brittle hardness and the eyes clear of the mesh of lines which even cosmetics had been unable to wholly disguise. Things he knew now must have been present. The hallmarks of her trade which, as a boy, he had failed to notice.

"My lord?"

"Leave me. All of you leave me."

They vanished like smoke and Dumarest sat alone on the emerald sward graced with the brilliant flowers beneath a gentle sky. Childhood. For others a time of pleasant memories. A dimly observed paradise inhabited by kind and helpful adults. But for him it had been a time of pain and terror and, after childhood had come the torment of reaching for maturity. The embarrassments of adolescence, the frustrations, the realization of inadequacy.

Was the Tau nothing but a gateway to hell?

"Hardy, my friend." The man who appeared next to him smiled in his whimsical fashion and gave a shrug. "But what is hell? All men, surely, create their own? And as they face the perils of an unfeeling universe, the careless indifference of fate, at least they have a defense. To laugh. To joke. To regard everything as a source of humor. Only so can we remain sane."

Jocelyn, ruler of Jest, a world afflicted with strange attributes. He, above all others, would know how to deal with incomprehensible situations.

"Not incomprehensible, Earl," he said. "Simply unfamiliar. But you'll understand when you have time to think. You'll understand."

"Of course you'll understand, Earl. It just takes application." Phasael, the handler of the ship who had taken a liking to the captain's protégé. Sitting now next to Jocelyn but not sharing his smile. "Hold the knife with your thumb to the blade and strike upward. Hit below the ribs and stick the heart. Even if you miss you'll lacerate the lungs and a man can't do much harm when he's drowning in his own blood."

"Blood." The physician shook his head. "It isn't enough, young man. "Blood alone won't save him. I'm afraid nothing can now."

And metal doors which had shut and a cold world on which he had to make his way.

Dumarest blinked, again suddenly alone, shivering a little from remembered chill, traces of snow thawing on his arms and shoulders.

Control.

He must maintain control!

A thought and it became real. Jocelyn, Phasael, the doctor who had attended the captain at the last. Scraps of memory given shape and form. Things which moved and talked and yet had no more real substance than a hologram. Ghosts from the past and all best forgotten.

But real. So real.

Dumarest looked at his boots, the knife thrust into the right, the texture of the material he wore. It had come with him, but no, that was impossible. Nothing had come with him. His clothing and body were elsewhere. Only his mind could have entered the Tau. Only his intelligence.

And yet?

He looked at his hand and, lifting the knife from his boot, rested the point against the flesh. A little extra pressure and the sharp point had drawn blood. A twist and with the blood came pain. A dream? If he should stab the blade into his heart surely he would die. Could men die in a dream?

"You are not in a dream, my darling." The voice sighed from the very air. "You are in a world strange but real. Be careful, Earl. Be so very careful."

Kalin? Lallia? Who had spoken? Dumarest stared around, seeing nothing but the rolling sward. A woman had warned him, words given life from fragments of memory, his own thoughts projected and given a weak semblance of reality. Had he concentrated, the speaker would have appeared, clothed in remembered flesh. Derai? Lavinia? The Matriarch herself? Had she, leaning over his unconscious body, breathed a warning? But in such intimate terms? Or had someone else spoken? The mother he had never known?

Dumarest looked at his hand, not surprised to find the minor wound had vanished. In a world where the mind ruled anything was possible. Even that a child who had grown into a young girl while sleeping could be found. But how?

On the horizon a point of light grew into a tremendous flare of released energies, thunder muttering as it grew, the noise increasing to match the blast of atomic destruction. Another, more, bursts of flame which traced the skies with flashing scintillations, patterns woven in coruscating brilliance, bright and gaudy colors spreading to blend and shatter to adopt new and more entrancing configurations.

A spectacle which had lasted for hours.

Sitting on the rolling plain, head bowed, mind aching from the strain of long concentration, Dumarest continued the show. The armies had marched, the combat craft lacing the skies, their weapons creating a threnody of awesome noise. Sound and light which he hoped would be noticed. A mock battle fought from the depths of his memory, given verisimilitude by his own experiences, set as a stage piece to attract a child.

Red set to strive against blue, yellow as an ally, green as a background, orange and purple and violet as minor instruments in the orchestration, swaths and strands of metallic colors to lace the whole into a composite pattern of noise and light which followed the dictates of his mind.

His mind—could it exist beyond his imagination?

And, even if she noticed it, would she be interested enough or curious enough to investigate its cause?

Then a flare died even as he brought it into being. A blaze of expanding light was snuffed and turned into a smoldering ember. A tide of pale cerise washed the sky bringing tranquility and silence.

A whirlpool spun in midair.

A swirling mass of luminous vapor which appeared and swept in diminishing circles to land before Dumarest and to remain a spindle of rapid motion from which sparkled little flashes of brilliance.

It moved toward him and he stepped back to find a wall halting his progress. A tall mass of chiseled stone which moved as he moved and halted when he came to rest. As the spindle advanced a shimmer grew before it, a barrier which halted it as the wall halted Dumarest. Then, abruptly, the whirlpool collapsed in a heap of sand and a man stepped forward and bowed.

"Greetings from Her Majesty the most noble and illustrious Queen Iduna, owner of this world and all within it, supreme head of the forces of good and evil, ruler of all things. Your name and disposition?"

Dumarest gave it, looking at the questioner, seeing a tall figure wearing bizarre armor, his face stern beneath a helmet. A dark, strong face, one cheek scarred, the mouth puckered, the eyes deep-set and darkly brown. A sword hung in a scabbard at his side.

"Earl Dumarest," the man said. "Lord of Earth and Defender of Right. What would you with my lady?"

"That I'll tell her."

"First you tell me." The man dropped his hand to the hilt of his word. "I am Virdius, Herald, Champion, a Lord of High Renown."

And, Dumarest guessed, a figment of an active imagination. A doll created by a child for her own amusement as had been the grandiose titles and adoption of power. Iduna, a child with a child's mind and a child's attention to detail. Of course a queen would have a champion—and what else would she be here but a queen? And who else would she respect but another claiming titles and rank of distinction?

A game it did no harm to play.

Dumarest said coldly, "The Lord of Earth does not bandy words with a mere underling. Tell your mistress that I crave audience. And remind her that she has seen a little of my power."

"A meaningless gesture. No rules had been set. No forfeit decided."

"I—"

"Have come to play wth my mistress and that is good. I hope that you can play better than the others. Now, for a beginning, you must win to the castle. I will be your guide. If you are beaten you must promise to pay a forfeit."

"And if I win?"

"Then you will be invited inside. It's a good game, Earl Dumarest, and one you'll enjoy. Say you'll agree."

"And if I don't?"

"Then you'll be a spoil-sport."

And perhaps lose his chance of meeting Iduna. If nothing else she would know the laws governing this place better than he and there was no point in putting off the meeting.

"I agree. How do I start? Which way is the castle?"

"It isn't your move yet," said Virdius seriously. "First the queen moves then you then her again. And you mustn't cheat. If you do you will spoil the game. Now, it's her move." He fell silent for a moment. "There!"

Dumarest felt the ground vanish from beneath his feet.

Chapter Seven

There was a moment of utter confusion, a sense of falling into an infinite darkness, then Dumarest turned, his boots hitting dirt, to see the sward had vanished to be replaced by the familiar black, volcanic sand. Grit which could hide lurking dangers and it changed as he looked at it into a field of solid ice.

"A good move," said Virdius. "You play well. I can tell that."

"By my first move?"

"Your second. First you stopped yourself falling then you changed the field into ice."

And Iduna turned it into water.

Dumarest sank, feeling the warm wetness lave his face, striking out to float as he considered the situation. A game of unknown rules yet he was getting the drift. A point he had to reach and one she would prevent him from making. Difficulties compounded and, if he should be unable to meet each new challenge with a defense, then she would have won. But what now? A boat to rescue him from drowning? A raft to lift him from the waves? To turn the sea into soil? A choice of almost infinite possibilities but once taken it would be her turn to move again and, if he was to play the game, she must be allowed to have it. But he must leave the sea. Like the sand it could hold too many dangers. But a raft could be grounded and a boat could be made to founder.

The log was safer.

It rested beneath his hands, rough, yet the bark not too rough to hold small but vicious insects, slimed but not slimed enough to make footing impossible. To Virdius he said, "In which direction lies the castle?"

"It rests in the place it occupies."

"Obviously. Where is that?"

"At the point where it is."

Riddles, yet the man was supposed to be his guide. Or maybe not. What had he said? "I am to guide you." Guide how? To what? Iduna, it seemed, had a peculiar sense of humor.

And it was her move.

The log rolled a little, began to pitch as a screaming wind suddenly lashed the water to foam. Lightning danced and sent clouds of vapor exploding from where it struck, the roar of thunder, the pounding impact of ceaseless explosions.

A storm which died as abruptly as it had started, to leave calm water and a shore edged with shining-leaved trees.

Trees which sprouted tendrils as Dumarest neared them, weaving coils of menace which changed into drooping fronds masking a rising landscape which turned into a crevassed slope emitting noxious fumes.

Which winds blew away.

Which gave birth to dragons.

Which vanished beneath a pall of snow.

Beyond the crest of the summit ran smooth ground dotted with copses and graced with the silvery thread of a river. A thread which carried the eye up and onward to the loom of somber mountains backing something which flashed like a tumbled handful of sparkling gems.

"The castle," said Virdius. "I said I would guide you."

To the final stages of the game. But the castle was far and it was the girl's move. Dumarest waited for it, confident he could take what she offered and counter it as he had done before. Playing a game no different in basic detail from that played by children everywhere with their verbalized use of objects—rock, paper, shears—each having power over another, each nullified by the correct pairing. A game she must have played often in the past.

When would she make her move?

Virdius said, "There is no obligation on her to make it. And if you move out of turn then you will have cheated and lost the game and must pay the forfeit."

A child?

Dumarest looked at the terrain, noting the greenness of the vegetation, guessing at the swampy nature of the ground it covered. To cover it would take time and effort and always would be the possibility of danger only avoided by his making a "move." And, if he did so, then he would have lost the game.

And?

The girl, sulking, would break all contact and, even if powerless to harm him, would remain beyond his reach. He could stay but to what end? And how long could he hope to survive? He remembered Muhi and how the man had looked while shambling around the compound. Of the others who had turned into distorted masses of wild tissue. Iduna was an exception—could he rely on being another? She had been a young child, her body still growing, able to adapt over the years. A girl, tended and cherished with loving care and given the best regardless of expense. He wasn't in the same category. Even now the Matriarch could be getting impatient and urging the technicians to experiment. How long had he been in the Tau?

He had no choice but to play the game as the girl dictated.

The ground was soft underfoot as he ran down the slope after memorizing the terrain. The softness, if he had judged correctly, would firm into a ridge of higher ground topped with vegetation less lush than the rest. It would take him to a clump of trees and then he had to take his chances to the river. Once he reached the water he would have gained a choice—to swim or walk. A choice he would make when he had to.

Water squelched beneath his boots and mud dragged at his ankles as Dumarest moved toward the higher ground. He was panting when he reached it and paused to rest, scraping rich black mud from his boots with quick movements of his knife. Virdius, unsullied, watched from one side.

As Dumarest sheathed his knife he said, "Are you staying with me all the way?"

"My duty is to guide you."

"And help?"

"To guide."

And perhaps more should Iduna so decide. Dumarest set off along the ridge slowing as he approached the clump of trees. Things could be lurking in the high branches and predators be waiting in the gloom of the undergrowth. To his relief there were neither and he studied the ground leading toward the river. It was thick with lush reeds, more soaring high at the edges of the stream. Stepping from the copse he

again felt the soft, yielding suck of mud and freed his boot
only with difficulty. Had he marched directly toward the river
he would be deep in the bog by now and forced to act to
save himself.

"If you consider yourself beaten I can accept your defeat,"
said the guide. "I doubt if the forfeit will be harsh."

"Don't you know? Haven't others had to pay the penalty?"

"Penalty?"

"Forfeit." A child's term for a child's game—but the punishment, even though decided on by a child, could be far
from childish. The young were often savage. "What is the
usual?"

"There is no strict rule. It depends on the moment. But
you must pay it if you lose and you will lose if you cheat."

"I haven't lost yet." Dumarest dived among the trees knife
lifted from his boot. "And I don't intend to lose."

A spur to make the girl use her move—once she did he
would give her no chance to make another, but she didn't fall
into the trap and Dumarest set to work on the trees. With the
blade he cut large sections of bark, some slender poles,
thicker branches together with a mass of thinly cut bark
which he wove into crude ropes. With them he lashed short
lengths of the thicker branches together, forming two frames
which he covered with sheets of bark. The rough construc-
tions lashed to his feet, he waddled toward the mud using the
poles to maintain his balance. Crude snowshoes which would
serve as well on soft ground, the extensions distributing his
weight over a larger area.

He was almost at the river when the creature struck.

It was long and low and with jaws parted to show the
gleam of serried teeth. A creature with clawed feet and a
weighted tail which ripped at the reeds as if it were a scythe.
Precariously balanced on the enlarged platforms Dumarest
caught the stir of reeds as the thing darted toward him, lifting
a pole to stab with it at the sloping head and eyes, to send
the tip into the mouth where it tore at the lolling tongue.

To go sprawling in the mud as the beast, snarling with pain
and anger, dashed against his leg.

The tail cut the air, jarring against his uplifted forearm,
ripping plastic and bruising the flesh beneath the protective
mesh. A blow which numbed and could have broken the limb

had not Dumarest yielded to it, using his arm as a shield to deflect the blow and send the tail whipping over his head. As the creature raced past he snatched at his knife, feeling the suck of mud as he moved, one hand trapped beneath him, the shoes on his feet hampering his legs. Bark and wood shattered as he drove one against the other, kicking to free his boots, slamming them wide against the soft and spongey ground as the weight of his body drove the mud higher around him.

Moments of furious activity as the beast slid to a halt, to turn on splayed paws, to lunge with jaws gaping wide to close on face and throat. Jaws which closed on the knife which Dumarest thrust into the open mouth, pint upward to transfix the palate as the hilt hit the loser jaw, saliva warm and sticky on the hand he kept clamped around the hilt.

Blood sprayed his face as the creature snarled in pain and rage, muscles jerking in his arm as it tore at the blade, the stench of its breath vile in his nostrils. For a moment the mud resisted the strength of the beast and Dumarest gritted his teeth, forcing himself to hold on, to use the beast which had tried to make him its prey. Pain made the animal back, legs stiffening, paws sinking as it struggled to rid itself of the torment in its mouth. Then it heaved, dragging Dumarest clear of the mud as it retreated toward the river, jerking itself free with torn jaws as he rolled over the edge to fall into the water.

To strike out and wash away the mud and blood and stench. To rest a while before following the thread of water toward the mountains and the castle.

It was something from a dream. A living jewel which flung a triple arch against the sky and graced with fluted towers and spires, turrets and cupolas set with drifting pennants and forked banners bearing bright devices. Light winked from crenellations; the gleam of armed and armored men watching from the battlements topping the high, gleaming walls. A moat held sportive fish which added brightness with their rainbow-leapings. A door shone with an inner effulgence and the drawbridge, lowered, shone like polished glass.

Light and brightness and all the colors from a children's story book. A building which followed no architectural discipline and would have been a hazard on any ordinary world.

The imagination of a child constructed in crystal and given solidity—the triple arch left no doubt as to whom that child must be. It would have been natural for Iduna to have copied the outstanding feature of her mother's palace.

"The castle," said Virdius. "The residence of Her Majesty. You have done well."

"More than well—I've won."

"Not as yet," corrected the guide. "You have yet to reach the castle. Beside the door, you see? A gong which must be struck by your hand. Only when you have done that will victory be granted."

He stood on the bank of the river, neat in his armor, his darkly handsome face impassive beneath the curved and pointed helmet. Standing in the water, Dumarest looked at him then at the castle. He was too low to see clearly but remembered the surround was of emerald sward which sloped from the bank to the moat. A surge and he was on land, dripping, little puddles collecting at his feet as he examined the approaches. Stepping forward he saw no advertised dangers.

Was winning to be so easy?

Halfway to the gong he heard the flap of wings and ducked as a bird, diving from a turret, suddenly darted at his eyes. A big, wide-winged creature which cawed and circled and came in again to attack his face. Again Dumarest ducked, rising with naked steel in his right hand, an edge which slashed to leave the bird flapping without a head, blood staining the grass.

"My move now, I think?"

"No, the bird is a natural part of the castle. The attack was not a calculated part of the game."

And how many more "natural" hazards would there be?

Dumarest stepped warily, watching for traps set in the grass; wires or snares triggered by the passage of his foot, even camouflaged predators trained to stay immobile until an intruder was within reach. The guide, he noted, had fallen behind him, his feet making no sound as they trod the sward.

Too easy.

It was all too easy!

Dumarest threw himself forward, turning in the air to hit the ground with his shoulders, seeing the splinter-bright flash of steel, the thin, vicious whine as the sword cut the air where he had been standing. A blow aimed to slash his legs and one delivered with enough strength to have cut them from his body. Beneath his helmet Virdius looked as impassive as before.

"You cheated!" Dumarest rolled as the blade tore grass and dirt at his side. "You've taken extra moves!"

"No, this move was incorporated in the first and that was when we met. Now it is being used."

An attack delivered without warning and one which would have crippled him and forced him to move which would have left the move to Iduna—how often had she played this murderous game before?

And how often was the guide permitted to attack?

Again steel whined through the air to touch the heel of his boot as Dumarest anticipated its fall, to roll and rise and parry the next swing, the thin, clear note of tempered metal rising as his knife met the longer sword. Longer and so more awkward to manipulate and a hindrance once an opponent was within the range of the point. Before the guide could shorten his blade Dumarest was on him, knife slamming up and into the face, the point shearing up a nostril, to smash through the sinus and into the brain. A blow aimed to kill.

One which would have killed an ordinary man but Virdius was far from that.

Backing he tore himself free of the blade and stood, his ruined face expressionless as again he lifted his sword, feet shifting to accommodate a lunge. Dumarest swayed as it came, felt the touch against his side and clamped his left arm down hard against the weapon, trapping it against his side. A step and his right hand darted forward with two rapid motions and this time Iduna had no choice. Either she moved or yielded her piece—a blinded man makes a poor warrior.

Then, as Dumarest watched, Virdius vanished.

He did it slowly, a fragment at a time, the face melting as if made of wax to shrink in a stream of sparkling vapor which wreathed about the helmet and left it empty. Then the armor itself, metal thinning to become gossamer and then to disappear to leave the remainder standing like a grotesque parody of what had been. Then, last of all, the sword joined the rest.

And from the door of the castle, came terror.

It filled the arched opening and swept over the drawbridge

in the shape of a glittering cloud of singing mist which spun and weaved and held faces which grimaced and held the attention while from it radiated a cold, merciless aura which chilled the blood and prickled the skin and filled the mind with all the horrors ever heard of ghosts and goblins and things which haunted the dark and swept down to eat the unwary and leave them mewing and unwanted in dismal places.

Iduna's move.

Her last.

The shimmering, singing mist condensed, lifted in a plume of vapor which poured into a bottle of purple glass which Dumarest corked and, holding it high, took one step and threw it hard against the gong.

As the brazen note died he passed into the castle in search of the girl.

She waited in a hall rich with tapestries, gemmed ornaments, tables loaded with succulent dainties, an army of dolls. Lights dazzled so that for a moment Dumarest could see nothing but reflected brilliance, then he caught the watchful presence of guards, of attendants, of an animal which rose bristling, of the woman who calmed it with a hand.

Shamarre who looked older and uglier than he remembered and who glared at him from her station at the foot of the throne.

On it sat a girl.

Dumarest studied her as he walked toward the dais narrowing his eyes against the brilliance of the jewels which adorned her, the glitter of the ornate crown. It rested on a mane of hair which seemed like liquid jet, each strand a filament of bright and shining loveliness. The face was a pale oval, the lips full and pouting, the eyes wide and graced by arched brows. The chin lacked strength as the body lacked maturity and the mouth resolution. As he watched she lifted a thumb and placed it within her mouth to suck as she watched his approach.

"That is close enough!" Shamarre was curt. "Halt and make obeisance to Her Majesty."

"Without looking at her Dumarest snapped, "The Lord of Earth does not take orders from underlings." Then, to the figure on the throne added harshly, "My lady—you cheated!"

The thumb lowered from the mouth.

"I did not!"

"The beast which attacked me close to the river—"

"Was a natural hazard. It was fair according to the rules. I did not cheat—so there!"

"A natural hazard," said Dumarest dryly. "As was the bird and the guide you sent me. A clever trick, my lady. I must congratulate you."

"I like to win," she said and giggled. "You looked so funny wearing those shoes and so startled when Virdius attacked. But you played well. Much better than the others. They didn't seem to know how to play at all. I'm glad you came here to join me. Would you like some tea and a cake?"

The cake was spiced and sweet and covered in thick, rich cream and he ate it in a small room seated at a table bright with the glitter of cups and plates and pots of solid gold. Others were at the table with himself and Iduna; a bear which stared with solemn, rounded eyes as it ate with delicate movements of a paw, a doll with a painted face which squeaked and scolded as it sipped, a dog with drooping ears which sat and watched and snapped thrown fragments from the air.

Iduna acted as the hostess.

"This tea is a special blend from Katanga," she said with adult pride. "I have galleys carrying it for me through the perils of the Juntinian Sea. And these cakes I baked myself using ingredients gathered from a dozen worlds. Teddy! Don't you be so greedy! Snap—here!" She smiled as the dog caught and swallowed a portion of cake. "When you've finished, Earl, shall we play another game?"

"Which?"

"Hide and seek?" She frowned. "No, not that one, not yet. How about armies? You take one side and I'll take the other and we have a war and the winner gets the other to pay a forfeit. Would you like to play that?"

"Later, perhaps."

"How much later?" She pouted her displeasure. "How long must I wait? We could play schools. I'll be the teacher and ask you questions and if you don't give me the correct answers I'll punish you." Then, as he made no comment, she added crossly, "Well, you think of a game."

"Questions," he said.

"What?"

"I ask you a question and you ask me one and we keep on until one of us can't or won't answer."

"And the loser pays a forfeit?"

"Yes." Then, as she frowned, he said, "Of course we could just talk. How long have you been queen?"

"A long time. I've always been the queen."

"Since you were a very small girl?"

"No—but since I came here. Are you really the Lord of Earth?"

"Why do you doubt it?"

"Earth. It's a funny name. Is there such a place? I mean really? Or is it something you just made up? I make up things all the time. Would you like some more cake?"

He took another piece and ate and watched the young yet oddly mature face of the girl he had come to find.

Girl?

At eleven many were women, ready and able to bear children, immature only in their minds. And Iduna had lived in the Tau for years. But she was the product of a rigid culture which set times and limits on those living within it. In such a society a child could remain that until puberty, then to become an infant, an adolescent and, only finally and usually after tests and rites, to be accepted as an adult.

He had known such worlds where men of thirty were still regarded as boys denied marriage and the chance of fatherhood. Others where girls were kept in seclusion until equally old then to lose their virgin status in an erotic ceremony. And yet others where boys became men as soon as they had killed and womanhood was determined by the swelling of a belly.

"Earl?"

"I was thinking." He smiled and took another bite of cake and felt the sickly sweetness fill his mouth. "Have you explored? Tried to find other lands?"

"What's the point?" She busied herself pouring tea. "Everywhere is the same. I took a raft once and went on and on and on and ended nowhere."

And had gone nowhere but he didn't mention that. She, as the oldest resident of the Tau, could teach him what he needed to know.

"Did you ever try to go back? To the palace, I mean. To your mother."

"No!"

"Your father, then?" The denial had been too sharp, too savage. A hate relationship? Such things were common between a neglected daughter and an ambitious mother. "You liked your father, didn't you? He played with you and showed you his things. Tell me some of the games you played. Did you ever hide in his study and spring out at him when he didn't expect it? Did he have friends call and talk and did you sit and listen?" He handed her the plate of cakes. "These are good."

"I know. I made them."

"You must teach me."

"Why? Don't you know how to cook? That's silly. All men can cook." Her disgust was genuine. "How are you ever going to hold a wife unless you can prepare her meals?"

"On Earth women do the cooking."

"Then Earth must be a funny place." She made no attempt to hide her lack of interest. "Can't you think of a new game we could play? Perhaps——" Her eyes veiled, became secretive. "Are you married?"

"No."

"Do you have a woman? I know many men have women they aren't married to. I've heard the servants talking. Are you a woman's lover?"

"No."

"Then are you one of——" Again she broke off, frowning before continuing, "You'd rather be with a man?"

"No. It's just that I'm here and you are the only female around and we aren't married and we certainly aren't lovers so how could I have either?"

"But there are other women here, Earl. You've seen some of them. Shamarre, Lydia, Wendy—lots of women. They come when you want them." Then, with a giggle, she added, "Men too. All kinds of men."

Toys for an erotic eleven-year-old child—but Iduna was no longer that age. Dumarest remembered the body he had seen. One belonging to a nubile young woman and she had spent years in the Tau where time need not match the pace of that outside. A day here could be an hour on Esslin. Time for imagination to develop and ancient needs to make themselves known. Time and the power to experiment free of the hampering restrictions of watching adults.

The face he saw now no longer belonged to a child.

"Men," she said again. "Such funny creatures, Earl. They come and they play as you want them to and then they go away. But you, you're different. You're not going away, are you? You're going to stay and play with me."

"I'll keep you company."

"Company? Is that the way you say it? Is that what you do when you play games?"

"There are other things than games."

"Such as?"

"We can talk and walk and examine things together. We can plan and discuss and find out about each other. We can explore. Did you and your father ever go exploring together?"

"Yes, sometimes when he could get away. We'd take a raft and go into the mountains and we'd find flowers and he'd tell me about them. And about other worlds too and the ways the people lived on them. At times he would hold me and that was good because he was so gentle and strong and I felt so safe. And he used to give me things. Tamiras said he spoiled me but I don't think I was spoiled."

"Tamiras?"

"A friend." She dismissed the subject. "What can we do together, Earl?"

"Explore. You mentioned Katanga and the Juntinian Sea. Where do they lie?"

"To the south. I made it that way. And the Burning Mountains lie to the north and the Eldrach Jungles to the west."

"And the east? What lies to the east?"

"Deserts," she said. "And the Place."

"The Place?" He frowned. "Just that? The Place?"

"Yes. I—yes, Earl. But that doesn't matter now. We can forget all about that. And forget the glaciers and the pits and the things I saw when . . . when. . . ."

"When you first came here?"

"Earl, it was horrible! I don't want to talk about it. I don't even want to think about it and you mustn't make me. Hold me, Earl. Hold me!"

And she was in his arms, clutching him tight as she buried her face against his chest, her shoulders quivering with remembered fears as she clung to the one real thing in her universe.

Chapter Eight

In the shadows a woman was moaning, her voice a gasping threnody of pain, thick, liquid, the gurgle of blood in laboring lungs turning the sounds into the mewing of a tormented beast. Kathryn turned toward it, feeling the tug and constriction of the transparent envelope she wore. A prophylactic measure the physicians had insisted she take and one she had not argued about. Hnaudifida was not a pleasant disease.

"Seven more cases in this area alone since the end of the storm, my lady." Sarah Magill gestured with an upraised arm. Her voice, muffled by the envelope she wore, was only slightly distorted by the diaphragms. "Another dozen suspected but we won't be certain until the end of the week. However all precautions have been taken as regards isolation."

"Separate quarters?"

"Of course."

"And full medical supervision?" If the unfortunates had the disease there was no hope but they should be given their chance. As the woman nodded Kathryn said, "How? How did they contract the disease? I ordered a total state of immobility. No movement between one estate and another and yet you have more cases here, others have been reported from previously clear areas, and there's talk of it even reaching the city itself."

"No slaves have left their work areas." Sarah was defiant. "And no overseers have left this estate. I can vouch for my own."

"But not for others, eh?" Kathryn met the other's eyes. "You've had visits? From whom?" Her voice hardened as the other hesitated. "I need to know, woman! This is an emergency!"

Outside the light was dying, strands of cloud drifting high against the emerald, thin wisps which formed moving pat-

terns of changing complexity. Kathryn stared at them, glad to
be out of the gloom, away from the scenes of pain and dis-
rupted bodily functions. She had been a fool, perhaps, to
have made the personal visit but anything was better than
just waiting and it did no harm to demonstrate her closeness
to the people and her interest in their troubles.

But it had not been pleasant to see the afflicted slaves
writhing on their cots, skins burning, lips cracked, fevered
eyes staring at her with the mute appeal of a stricken beast.
What had the monk said?

There, but for the grace of God, go I!

And, but for an accident of birth, she too could have been
a slave, born to serve without question, living the span of her
days in a manner chosen by others. A bad thought which she
dismissed as a technician sprayed the envelope with sterilizing
fluids and later helped her out of it when they were safely
high and on their way back to the palace.

Gustav was waiting and anxiety made him sharp.

"You were stupid, Kathryn. You should not have gone to
visit the sick. The risk was too great."

"There was no risk. All precautions were taken."

"Did you filter every cubic inch of air between here and
there? Made sure you touched no part of the raft? Floated on
the ground? How can you claim you took no risk?"

He was becoming foolish. She snapped, "I did what I considered best and that's all there is to it. A ruler has certain re-
sponsibilities and I had to demonstrate my concern. Have you
correlated all the data? Good. Your conclusions?"

She frowned as he gave them. From the first reported case
the increase and progression were frightening. On every estate
there were slaves in the terminal period and others were sus-
pect. A natural progression but what had caused the sudden
outbreak? And why was it so widespread?

"I suspected a carrier," said Gustav. "Such are rare but not
unknown and so I checked on all movements from ten days
before the first case until now. A waste of time, I'm afraid;
the movements of slaves can be found but not those of overseers and certainly not those of owners and nobles."

"An importation?"

"It would seem it has to be. No disease is suddenly created
and there has to be a reason for the outbreak. I checked all
ship arrivals and visitors. Most stayed in the city to conduct

their business. Tanya Ell had a guest stay with her for ten days and Marion Cope a visit from her nephew. He is still with her as far as I can gather. Aside from the consignment of slaves brought by Hylda Vroom that is all." He added dryly, "Esslin is hardly a tourist attraction."

"Don't make jokes, Gustav!"

"No. I apologize, my dear. Was it bad?"

"Worse than I thought. A sick woman lacks dignity and a dying one begins to lack all the attributes of humanity. The men—" She broke off, shuddering. "Hnaudifida makes no sexual distinction."

And was no respector of persons. Now the slaves, soon the overseers and free residents of the estates, then the nobles and owners. She thought of the city filled with dead and dying, creatures who dragged themselves over the stones, burning, begging for water, rotting even as they begged.

There, but for the grace of God, go I!

"Kathryn?" Gustav was staring at her. "You said?"

"Nothing." She must have sub-vocalized the words or whispered them—what did it matter? "Run the data through the computer again and make sure the technicians are doing their job. Check on all known movements since the ban. Most don't think it applies to any but slaves. Sarah Magill had visits from Maurneen Clairmont, Ina Hine, Arora Kochbar and Tamiras."

"Tamiras?"

"He went out there to test the geological structure for a proposed installation or something. Check it out. All the visits were within the last few days. See if there is a correlation. There has to be a common factor. It's the only explanation for the widespread distribution and increase of the disease. Find it for me, Gustav. Please."

"I'll find it," he promised. "But on one condition." He smiled at her expression. "Nothing too serious. I just want you to promise never to do anything as foolish as visiting the dying again. Yes, foolish," he repeated sharply as she lifted a hand in protest. "What if you fall ill? Die?"

"Would it matter?"

"To me, yes. To Esslin, certainly. And what of Iduna?"

"Perhaps I would be with her."

"But you would have left me." He stepped closer, one hand lifted to touch her cheek, the fingers tracing a path to her lips. Fingers which kissed as they moved. "And if you leave me, my dearest," he whispered. "What have I left? You promise?"

She nodded. It was good to have someone to make decisions at times. Someone who cared.

Tamiras said, "This is ridiculous. Gustav, if we weren't old friends I'd take offense at the implication. To even imagine that I could be responsible for such a thing is beyond reason. Why, for God's sake? What reason could I have for spreading hnaudifida?"

"I didn't say that!"

"You implied it."

"No, I was merely checking out certain data. Looking for a common factor which would give a lead of some kind to the cause and spread of the sickness." Gustav gestured at the papers littering his desk. He looked strained, dark circles of fatigue magnifying the brilliance of his eyes, but held himself with an unexpected firmness. "A job which needs to be done and I am doing it."

"Why you? Why not the technicians?"

"Must we always rely on others? As I remember it, Tamiras, you are always becoming personally involved with your rafts and crews and equipment. Why not leave it to your technicians?"

"A man can only trust himself." Tamiras shrugged, then smiled. "You've made your point, Gustav. And, by doing this, you feel closer to Kathryn, right?"

A man shrewder than he at first appeared. The straggle of beard distracted the attention from the set of the lips and line of jaw, the creases of resolve and the directness of the eyes which, at times, held the impact of spears. A clever man— why did he stay on Esslin? A son of an exile who owned no lands and no fine houses. Who made his way on a pension granted by Kathryn in an effort to heal the breach caused by his rebellious parent. A warped genius who worked in the field of electron magic and who could easily find fame and backers on other worlds.

But he was no longer young and other worlds could never be home and on Esslin he had respect and as much fame as a man could ever be granted. And more freedom than most.

Now he said quietly, "I know how it is, Gustav. The frus-

tration of being always regarded as an inferior. Women think
of us as children, irresponsible boys who have no concept of
the duties attending maturity. They give us our toys and, as
long as we are good, tolerate us and our eccentricities. Even
my own mother never really understood the importance of
my work. And even though I've proved my ability a dozen
times, who will give me their trust? I make field-baths and
talk of electronic dirt removers and am allowed to construct
household utensils. But when I demonstrate that I have the
knowledge to master the climate I am shunned. No man must
ever be allowed to become too powerful. Not on Esslin."

"Give it time, Tamiras. Things will change."

"Time? I have no time! I—" Tamiras broke off, lips pursed
beneath his beard, looking at hands which trembled. When
they were still he said blandly, "We digress, old friend. It is
good that a husband wants to help his wife and I am the last
to decry your motives. Even though by helping her you set
the yoke more firmly about your neck. Now, as to my movements, they are simply explained. I went to check the geological substrata in various areas and to take measurements of
the planetary magnetic field at certain selected points. I also
took sightings as to elevations and elementary dispositions of
any heights in those regions. If you wish I can let you have
my scheduled plan of operations which includes dates, times,
findings and comments. Had I expected your accusation I
would have brought it with me."

"There has been no accusation," said Gustav. "This is an
investigation, no more. But I will be pleased to check your
records. Would they, by any chance, include details of any
others you may have met during your journeys?"

"I keep records, Gustav, not a diary. How do I know what
others might have done? One thing I am certain about however is that none of them would have wanted to spread
sickness in the land. What could they gain by it? Their own
property is at risk; with the harvest so close they will need
every slave they can get to work in the fields." He added
thoughtfully, "Of course, there is one remote possibility, but I
hesitate to mention it."

"Possibility?" Gustav frowned. "You mean you have suspi-
cions of someone who could be responsible?"

"Not that. Not exactly. I was thinking more on the lines of
an unsuspecting carrier."

"That has been checked. None of the residents of the afflicted areas are or could be carriers. The outbreak is recent, a resident carrier would have been spotted long ago."

"Recent—so who has come to Esslin within the immediate past? Visitors? Relatives? And what of Hylda Vroom's slaves?"

"You cover old ground. I've checked. In any case the slaves arrived after the first reports of the sickness."

"Which leaves us what?" Tamiras frowned in thought. "Who else? Who could have arrived and—" He looked up to meet Gustav's eyes. "The monks."

"The monks? No!"

"Why not? Oh, I'm not talking about a deliberate attempt to spread infection, I'd be the first to defend them from that accusation, but what about a carrier? A man who doesn't even know he carries hnaudifida and spreads it in sheer ignorance."

"A monk—but his companions?"

"Could be immune. It happens, Gustav, and on other worlds they may not be as prone to the disease as we are here on Esslin. Mind you, I make no accusation. It is a possibility and perhaps a remote one. But it could be the answer."

"No." Gustav shook his head. "You're forgetting something. They have been here for some time now—if one was a carrier then why has the disease taken so long to show itself."

"The carrier could be a recent arrival."

"And the rest?" Gustav moved some of his papers, selected one, ran his eyes over the list of figures. "The monks stay in the city close to the field. How could they have been in contact with slaves residing on distant estates and so far apart from each other? The thing is impossible."

Tamiras said, "The Festival. You're forgetting the Festival."

The three-day period when harsh discipline was relaxed and carnival prevailed. A safety valve to release pent up emotions, anger and resentment allowed to boil away in dancing and drunken orgies and wild abandon. A time in which the wise kept to their homes and only the guards were out in force.

"The Festival," said Tamiras again. "The monks were here before it and the contacts could have been made then." Casually he added, "And don't forget that one of the monks died. It might be interesting to find out from what."

The body had gone, converted into ash and basic constituents and returned to the universe from which they had been formed. Brother Juba was now nothing but a memory and the work which three had handled must now be completed by two. But not for long. Already replacements were on the way now that the Church had received grudging permission to establish itself on Esslin. The first pecarious foothold which must be strengthened with younger blood and more resilient sinew.

The cycle which Remick had experienced before but now doubted if he would again. He would stay—few monks ever retired to spend their last days in the beautiful tranquility of Pace where they served to the last in bringing comfort to those tormented by mental anguish or physical pain. He would stay and Brother Echo would stay and they would die here on this world and be burned and remembered for a while and then forgotten as those memories were erased by time.

But something of them both would remain as something of Juba would linger. A hand lifted to strike and then lowered with the intended victim untouched, a degree of tolerance intended where none had been evident before, a moment of concern for another instead of blank indifference—these things would be their monument.

To the guards who came to close the church he said, "What is this? We have the permission of the Matriarch."

"Shut up!" The back of the woman's hand bruised his lips in a casual blow. "Where is the body of the one who died?" She scowled when he told her. "Burned? How about his effects?"

She collected them as he watched, hands deft within their gloves, her bulk taut in places against the transparent membrane which covered her. A garment Remick had seen before and he restrained Echo as the man began to protest.

"Leave them, Brother."

"But Juba! His things!"

Scraps and pieces without intrinsic worth. A piece of well-rubbed stone which he had found when a lad and found a tactile pleasure in its contact. A faded smear of pigments which could have been the likeness of a woman's face or the abstract swirls of a fevered brain. A pocket maze with little steel balls running in an elaborate pattern of garish colors. A kaleidoscope. A device for producing bubbles from soapy water. A pair of hand puppets. A lip-flute. A book filled with entrancing pictures.

Juba had always liked children.

Remick watched as they were thrown into a sack, the small accumulation which was the sum total of a life. As the guard straightened he said quietly, "How bad is it?"

"What?"

"The sickness. How bad is it?"

A question Gustav answered later when, leaving the church and Echo under guard, the woman bustled him to a room in the palace.

Gustav also wore a prophylactic membrane as did the medical technicians who came to take samples of blood and tissue from the unresisting monk. As they left Gustav gestured to a table bearing wine and small cakes.

"Eat and drink if you wish. This may take a little time."

To starve and thirst would accomplish nothing. Remick helped himself to a cake and goblet of wine. The cake was scented with a delicate fragrance, the wine held body and warming strength.

"A disease," he said. "I had heard rumors but nothing was certain. How bad is it?"

"Bad enough. How did the other monk die?"

"Juba? He was old."

"And age killed him? That alone?"

"It helped." Remick did not mention the rough handling of the guards. "He was not diseased, brother. You have my assurance on that."

"How can you be sure? Living as you do, moving from one poverty-stricken area to another, eating when you can, always in contact with the sick—you recognize the possibility?"

Remick said quietly, "Hnaudifida has an incubating period of six days. The first symptoms are headaches, fatigue, lassitude and irritation. Then comes a mild fever and aching of the joints. The first eruptions usually become manifest on the softer regions of the body: the armpits, the groin, the insides of elbows and knees. Sometimes on the face and neck. After four days the lassitude has increased to a point where voluntary movement is resisted and the fever rages with a higher intensity. The eruptions spread and form oozing ulcers. There is a general loss of bodily fluids. The patient becomes incontinent and care must be taken to see that vomit is not sucked into the lungs. After the second week death is inevitable. How many cases have been reported to date?"

"Thirty-nine."

"Isolated?"

"Yes, thank God."

"Slaves?" Remick had expected the nod. "You may expect another two hundred percent to fall sick and of those about fifteen percent will recover if given the proper care. They will then be immune to hnaudifida." Pausing he added, "As Brother Juba was immune. As both Brother Echo and I are immune."

"You have all had the disease?"

"No, nor many others we have been innoculated against. Surely, brother, you did not think the Church so irresponsible as to send devastation among others. No monk is a carrier. All monks have been protected as far as medical science will allow against a variety of ills. How else can we do our work treating the sick?"

A thing Gustav should have known. A thing he should have guessed and yet why should he have suspected? How well did he know the monks? They came and worked among the poor and it was hard to remember that they were products of a high technology which used all knowledge and skills to achieve efficiency. He remembered things he had heard; of the long training each monk had to undergo, the conditioning and indoctrination and acquiring of ability. The poverty they displayed was real, a defense against the sin of pride, for only by rejecting possessions could they give full attention to their supplicants.

A man who has nothing has nothing to lose. And having nothing to lose has everything to gain.

Such a man could be envied.

Gustav said, "I must apologize for the inconvenience you have been caused. But, for the duration of the emergency, your church must remain closed."

To his surprise the monk didn't object. Instead he said, "Perhaps we could be of help. As we are immune we could

tend the sick—it will do no harm to bring them together.
Also we could help to develop vaccines to save those who
have been at risk. I have knowledge of the techniques and
would be pleased to work with your technicians if they
agree."

They would agree, argue though they might at first, but
Kathryn would see that they obeyed his orders. And the
monk had given him confidence that the outbreak could be
controlled. The man was so calm, so self-assured. A man
confident of his strength as Dumarest had been.

Dumarest!

Why had he been such a coward as to allow the man to
take his place?

Chapter Nine

The wind was from the south, blowing from Katanga over the Juntinian Sea, a breeze loaded with fragrance which stirred the leaves of blooming trees and caused their multi-colored fruits to swing and turn in random motions. Blooms and fruits on the same tree and all the blooms fully open, all the fruits at a perfection of ripeness.

When you owned a universe all things were possible.

Dumarest halted, breathing deeply, looking over a conception of paradise. Ground which felt like a soft mattress covered with thickly piled carpet. Air scented with a dozen perfumes. Trees and bushes covered with blooms and fruits, nuts and berries of all imaginable hues, shapes and flavors. The moat with its fish. The castle which dominated all.

Iduna's universe.

It had to be hers. No one but a child or someone with a childish mind would want such a profusion of gaudy colors and sweetness and fairy-tale appurtenances. A refuge she had made for herself against the alien terrors which had greeted her when entering the Tau. He remembered the way she had clung to him, her tears, the abject fear of remembered horrors. Remembered too his own experiences and wondered how the sanity of a child could have prevailed.

"Earl!" Iduna waved to him from the battlements, streamers of fluttering silk adding to the luster of her hair. "Earl, come and join me!'"

A command?

If he ignored it would she send guards to make him prisoner? Could they hold him against his will? Would she change the environment to send him wandering in a maze? But here in the Tau he had an equal power and no matter what move she made he could counter. A game—was everything here a game?

"Earl! Hurry!"

A thought and he could be standing at her side but habit made him turn toward the castle, to enter it, to find a flight of sweeping stairs and run up to the first balcony, the second, to halt on the third and open a door.

And stared into a swirling chaos.

Mist which held barely discerned form, which writhed, which screamed in a thin, droning cacophony, which chilled with numbing terror.

A thing trapped, suffering, locked in a living hell.

A moment and it was gone, the door now giving on to a chamber soft with hanging tapestries, bright with sunlight streaming through narrow windows fitted with stained glass so that the beams made bright patterns on the tessellated floor. An empty room which held nothing but the furnishings and the light.

"Earl!" Iduna, impatient, calling to him from the balcony above. "Quickly, Earl!"

A new game she wanted to play and play it immediately with the arrogance of one unaccustomed to waiting. Or perhaps she wanted to show him something as a child would demand attention before displaying a scrawled painting or other adults to watch as a trick was performed. And it seemed, always, she hated to be alone.

The battlement was thronged with soldiers, attendants, Shamarre watching silently from her station, the beast at her side. Colors and brightness and figures which moved and faces with eyes and mouths which talked and yet all was nothing more than an extension of the castle, the battlement, the curtain walls, the triple arch and the turrets. Props to bolster a play.

And the thing screaming in the mist?

It had been real and he had seen it; of that Dumarest was certain. A glimpse into something ugly behind the glittering façade. A part of the castle, perhaps, for castles contained dungeons and not all prisons were below the ground. Yet it had changed in a flash into something else. A room harmless enough and one to be expected behind the door he had opened.

A glimpse of hell in paradise.

"Iduna!" She turned as he called and he saw her face illuminate with pleasure. "What is it? What are you going to show me?"

"You guessed!"

"No, but am I right? Is there something you want me to see?"

For answer she lifted her arm, pointing and, in the distance he could see wheeling shapes against the sky. Birds or things shaped like birds then as they came closer he could see things of nightmare, shapes elongated, distorted, set with tormented faces and disjointed limbs. Objects which keened as they wheeled.

"I made them," Iduna said proudly. "Shamarre!"

The beast at the woman's side sprang to the battlements and stood for a moment on a crenellation, its body sharply etched against the sky. A moment only then it sprang into empty air, to hang as if suspended for a moment, then to fall as wings sprouted from his shoulders. Wide, curved, fretted pinions which caught the air and gave the beast mastery over the element as it swept to the attack, paws extended, claws gleaming like sickles. Talons which ripped and tore as the beast closed with the flying horrors and sent their blood flying in a carmine rain.

A brief and savage conflict which sent the nightmare shapes to litter the ground as the beast, jaws, muzzle and paws smeared with gore, came to rejoin Shamarre. She patted it as it crouched at her feet, busy washing itself, the wings vanished from the smooth, tawny hide.

"Earl?" Iduna was looking at him, the smooth, round face smiling, changing even as he watched, to betray something feral. "You like that, Earl?'

'"Why?"

"Why?" A frown ruined the smoothness of her forehead. "Why what? What do you mean?"

"Why the display? The butchery?"

"The combat, you mean." Dignity stiffened her voice, the offended pride of one who has never been questioned as to her motives. "It was sport. The chase." Then, as he made no comment, added, "Don't you like to hunt?"

"No. Neither do I like to see others kill for pleasure. There was no need. Those things didn't threaten you in any way. They—" He broke off, remembering. The things had been created with a thought and had no greater reality than the castle, the beast which had killed them, the attendants and guards standing now on all sides listening to the argument. He must not display his condemnation. It would serve no useful purpose and would alienate the girl. He said mildly, "I am sorry. You tried to please me."

"In my castle," she said stiffly, "all guests are entertained. And within my walls you are safe from the dangers which wait outside. You were foolish to have wandered away from the protection I offer. Those things I made and had destroyed, they were modeled on things which live in the outer marches. It is fatal to be caught by them at night."

Night?

Dumarest glanced at the sky seeing the same, flame-shot expanse he had seen before. But it had changed more than once and was changing again, growing darker and seeming to hold menace as it did so.

"Come," Iduna ordered. "It grows chill."

A thin wind gave truth to the statement. Dumarest saw others shiver, a servant draping a cloak around Iduna's shoulders, felt a sudden bite in the air. Things which made the castle seem a greater haven. As the gloom thickened flambeaux cast a warm and flickering light from cressets set on walls and turrets.

"Come," said the girl again. "Earl, you will have time to bathe before dinner."

A servant guided him to his room, a soft-eyed woman with a crest of fine, blonde hair and round eyes of vivid blue. Her thin garment was of silk and lace and did little to hide the smooth curves of what it covered. Her arm when Dumarest touched it was warm, the creamy skin gilded with a fine fuzz of hair.

"My lord?"

"What is your name?"

"Irenne, my lord."

"How long have you been here?"

"Here, my lord? Why, all my life. It is an honor to serve Her Majesty." Her eyes met his, unswerving. "And any who are the guests of the Queen."

"Do you have many? Guests, I mean. Can you remember names? Nerva? Charles? Fhrel?" Names Gustav had given him. Those belonging to the volunteers who had gone before.

"Muhi?" He thought he saw the flicker of her eyes. "Muhi? Do you remember him?"

"No, my lord. Your bath is beyond that door. Is it your wish that I attend you?"

"No."

Alone Dumarest examined the bathroom. It was what he had expected. A sunken tub fashioned of marble, the taps and appointments of gold. Fluffy towels hanging on a warming rack. Soap and lotions dispensed by crystal containers. The light was a soft amber and the air reeked of perfume. Walls, floor and ceiling were unbroken mirrors.

Lying in the water Dumarest looked at his reflection. His face seemed younger than it had, small lines vanishing and marks of old stresses gone to reveal a smoother visage. The scar tissue was gone beneath the line of his hair and the scars of other, older wounds were no longer to be seen.

His doing?

Iduna's?

Was he as she saw him or as he wanted to be? A question he pondered while lying in the steaming water enjoying its liquid caress. She had created the castle and everything in it and he was now in the castle. He thought of the servant, Irenne. She had seemed real and warmly human. Her body had radiated a feminine warmth and had certainly been made of flesh and blood. A real woman with a life of her own and memories which were wholly hers and loves and hopes and ambitions too, perhaps. As Shamarre was a real woman copied from memories of her mother's guard, one who could have acted as a nurse at times. A figure of known and trusted strength.

Did the others also model those she had known years ago? Guards and attendants and servants all duplicated here in the Tau to continue familiar duties?

Riddles which could wait. Solving them would solve nothing for the real problem remained. How to restore Iduna to the real world where her mother waited to take her into her arms. Where his own body now lay helpless among those who had no cause to concern themselves over his welfare.

How long had it been?

Time had lost all meaning, lost in an eternal day now, for the first time, broken by night. A darkness induced by Iduna's whim or a natural part of her universe. A time of potential danger when it would be comforting to be behind thick walls patroled by trusted guards. Not all pleasures were things of silken comfort.

And yet could danger, real danger, exist here?

Dumarest stretched and watched the run of water over his arms and chest, little rivulets which traced individual paths as they broke from the main flood. Water which felt and tasted and acted as if real. Which was real—and if real then a man could drown in it.

But what was reality?

If a thought could make a thing then was that thing more than thought? In the world of the Tau nothing was tangible and how could intangibility affect the same?

And what of the screaming thing he had seen?

An enemy trapped and tortured and left forgotten in the mist as Iduna concerned herself with the novelty of a new playmate? Leaning back Dumarest closed his eyes and tried to remember each minor detail. The door had opened and he had looked into hell. A chaos of mind-wrenching horror which had vanished even as seen but the impact had remained. The face—where had he seen that face before?

A moment then he opened his eyes and shook his head. The glimpse had been too short, the impact too shocking and details now were added items won from personal memory. But he could try again.

Rising he reached for a towel then dropped his hand. A thought should dry him so what need of a towel? But the thought wasn't enough and, still wet, he tried again. Losing patience he rubbed himself dry and moved back into the other, larger room. It held a wide bed, small tables heavy with crusted objects of enticing shape and color, a lamp which threw circling patterns of variegated hues. The air held a delicate scent he hadn't noticed before and a window, sealed, held a pattern of stars.

The door opened at his touch to show a corridor lit with flaring torches, the floor decorated with a profusion of inlaid leaves so that he seemed to be walking on a forest path, the walls to either side carved to resemble massive boles from which tiny faces seemed to peer and wink and grin. A path which curved to a balcony from which stairs ran up and down. To where a guard stood in frozen immobility, her face rigid and hands set on the shaft of a pennoned lance. As

Dumarest passed her eyes remained fixed; scraps of broken glass gleaming in the shadow of her helm; a casque painted red and orange in the dancing flames of flambeaux.

The silence was absolute.

Dumarest paused at the balcony looking up one flight of stairs then the other to where torches danced and guards stood like statues at their stations. He turned, suddenly, eyes probing the corridor, conscious of someone watching but seeing nothing. The passage was deserted and only the shadows moved from the dancing interplay of light. Like the corridor the stairways were barren of life other than the guards and they could have been made of stone. The air changed to hold the stench of corruption.

A stench which grew as Dumarest hesitated on the balcony trying to orient himself. To determine how to find the door which had given on horror.

The third balcony up—that he remembered, but on which floor was his room? Down a flight? Up in a turret? Was even the stairway the same? The interior of the castle was a maze in which it would be easy to get lost. Which way? Which?

Dumarest began to climb, guessing that his room was on the second floor, using the basis of the guess as the node of a frame of reference. Up a flight then and turn left and the door facing him should be the one he wanted.

But there was no door, only a blank wall of stone before which a guard stood in rigid immobility.

The guard and the stench was now sickening.

Another flight and this time there was a door but it opened on a chamber dark but for the illumination cast by a single candle, unfurnished but for a single chair. Higher there was a salon flanked with windows which showed the night, stars like gems which glowed with indifferent interest and formed patterns he did not know. The air was cleaner now and he used it as a scent, tracing it back and down until it filled his nostrils and mouth with the stink and taste of vileness.

To the blank wall and the immobile guard.

Back in his room Dumarest crossed to the window and studied the panes. They were false; the entire window was one sheet of glass crossed with leaden strips so as to emulate individual segments, the glass itself firmly set in a rigid frame. To open it would require partially demolishing the surrounding wall.

Would a child know of the intricacies of glazing, masonry, joinery? Was there need?

And astronomy?

Dumarest reached toward the stars depicted on the window. His fingers seemed to touch them, a common illusion, but the perspective was wrong, the stars seeming more like discs scratched at random on a sheet of heavily smoked glass than true suns burning in the void. And space held more than stars. There should be the blur of distant nebulae, the shimmer of fluorescence from electronically activated curtains of gas, the somber loom of clouds of dust—all the awesome splendor of the universe.

"What are you doing, Earl? Looking for Earth?"

Turning, he looked at Iduna. She was no longer a child.

The door creaked a little as she closed it behind her to step into the chamber. Tall, smiling, hair a glinting mass of liquid ebon, the midnight tresses shot with sparkling white fire from trapped diamonds. Fire matched by the stones around her throat and wrists and narrow waist. Cold brilliance which sparkled from the brooch on the simple black gown which hugged prominent breasts as it fell to be caught at the narrow waist, to swell over the hips and thighs, to trail the floor. A gown slit down the side so as to reveal the alabaster whiteness of calf and knee and thigh, the delicate, high-arched feet nursed in sandals of diamond-studded ebon.

"My lady!"

Her regal stance earned the title but there was more. Her face, whiter than he remembered, was a vision of loveliness, the lips full, the cheeks shadowed with slight concavities, the bone prominent, the eyes wide and enigmatic beneath thin and slanting brows. Gone were the irresolution, the petulance, the immaturity. Standing before him was a woman.

"Earl!"

"My lady?" He had forgotten what she had said. A question?

"I asked if you were looking for Earth." Her voice was the music of the wind, the pulse of an organ. Bells chimed in distant cadences and her very breath scented the air. "Earth," she repeated. "Your home world or so you said. Don't you remember? Earl!"

He was standing staring like a stunned and bewildered boy.

With an effort he looked away, his eyes resting on the lamp, the table, the wide bed—it was impossible not to look at the woman. Closing his left hand he felt the bite of nails against his flesh and clenched the hand tighter.

"My home world, my lady, yes." He drew a deep breath. "It is far from here. I don't know where."

"It can be found." She was casual, the subject was already boring her. "My father could help you if necessary. He is fond of old things and puzzles and mysteries and problems. They help to occupy his time."

"Your father? Gustav—"

"I have only one father, Earl. Is it possible to have more than one?"

"No. I don't think it is."

"Then why ask stupid questions." The movement of a hand put an end to the discussion. "Now tell me how I look. You like the gown? The gems?"

"You are lovely, my lady. More than lovely. You are the most beautiful woman I have ever met. The most beautiful there ever could be. Even to look at you makes me the happiest of men."

"You may be happy, Earl." She was gracious. "And because you have been so kind there is no need of formality. Your Queen permits you to address her as an equal. An honor given to few. Now you may kiss my hand."

Dumarest took it, bowing his head over it as he lifted the fingers to his lips, to touch the satin-soft whiteness, to taste the sweet effulgence, the breath the exuded perfume. A scent which triggered a sudden, near-overwhelming desire so that he burned to take, to hold, to possess—he tasted blood as his teeth bit at the inner membranes of his cheek.

Was he mad to lust after a child?

Not a child. Never a child. Iduna was all woman and fully mature and her presence filled the chamber and stimulated his every cell with an aching need to take her and use her in the ancient ceremony of procreation. He wanted her more than life itself. To be apart from her was unthinkable. He felt like kneeling before her to kiss her feet, to cringe, to grovel, to beg.

What was happening to him?

"Earl!" Her laughter was sweet and echoed in a fading tintinnabulation. "You look so odd. So startled. And there is blood on your lips. What's the matter? Haven't you ever played this game before?"

Game?

Of course, what else would it be to her but a game? One played many times with figments of her imagination, men created to act a part, to move and talk and act as she directed. To be consumed with a burning passion and an undying love. To worship even as they lusted and the lust itself touched with gentle regard. Emotions which had no place in reality. A lover manufactured from the stuff of girlish dreams.

But he was no puppet and this was a game he had played many times before.

He said, "You're cheating again, Iduna. That perfume has aphrodisiacal qualities. Pheronomes?"

"What?" Her ignorance was genuine. "What are they?"

"Biological cues. Produced and emitted to gain a predicted response. Certain insects use them to attract mates." He watched her face as he spoke, the movements of her eyes. "Have you never heard of them?"

"No. Earl—you mustn't say I cheat. That is unkind and you must never be unkind." She stepped toward him, all darkness and flashing gleams of silver light, her perfume wafting before her like a herald announcing the approach of beauty. And she was beautiful. More than beautiful. "Earl! Earl, my love!"

He felt the touch of fingers on his hair and realized that he was on his knees before her, hands lifted to clasp her thighs, face pressed against the join of her limbs. A warm, soft and endearing merging of curves which radiated a sensual heat and caused his blood to thunder in his ears.

"Iduna!"

"My love. My darling. Earl, I need you." Her fingers burned like a sweet flame. "I want you, my darling. I want you."

Seduction, fined and honed and rendered irresistible, his own yearnings working against him to construct a creature which epitomized all loveliness and all beauty ever dreamed of by lonely men cringing in the cold hostility lurking between the stars. A woman who loved and cared and who wanted to give. And give in the way so dearly wanted and do it without instruction or hesitation or all the numbing preliminary rituals with which all such meetings were cursed. To be everything he had ever dreamed of.

"Earl!"

To fill his life, his universe, his brain and heart and body, to become his every thought, his every cell.

"Earl!"

To dominate him. To rule absolutely. To overwhelm utterly.

Yet to surrender held such sweet temptation.

"No!"

"Earl? What is wrong, my darling?"

"No!" He backed and forced himself to stand away from her. His head spun and he felt dizzy as the swirling hues of the lantern painted a cloud of drifting rainbows over stone and floor and roof and bed. A thought and it would steady—but it did not. A thought and the girl would vanish—but she remained. And that was wrong for in the Tau thoughts were master.

"No, Earl," she said and came toward him, smiling, tints of color against the smooth cascade of her hair. "This is my world. I made it and everything it contains obeys me. Everything, Earl."

He remembered the water which had not dried, the stars which hadn't moved—and suddenly his ears were filled with the thin, horrible screaming of the face he had seen in the mist. His face?

"Darling." Iduna was close now, her breasts touching his chest, her face warm before him, the perfume of her breath strong in his nostrils. "Shall we get on with the game?"

Chapter Ten

There had been headaches and fatigue and irritation and, later, a fever and aching of the joints but, thank God, it had not been hnaudifida.

"You are sure?" Gustav looked at the report in his hand, seeing the notations and knowing what they signified but wanting reassurance. "There is no doubt?"

"None." The technician was patient. "We've run treble checks, my lord, and there is no possibility of error. The Matriarch had a chill and a slight infection which has already responded to treatment. A short rest and she will be as fit as ever." She smiled at the relief on his face; it was good that a man should be concerned for his wife. "Would you care to see her?"

She sat propped in a wide bed, the air tainted with the odor of antiseptics slight but unmistakable beneath the perfume. Her favorite, he noted, the clear, crisp scent of pine which became her so well. The open suited her, the rolling plains and forests and mountains. A creature of the wild tamed and channeled but never wholly free of the spaces which called her their own. A fanciful impression but one he nurtured as compensation for the cramped life of the city.

"Kathryn?" She was awake and opened her eyes as he came to sit beside her. "You're looking well."

A banality and a lie—she seemed shrunken and smaller in the face than she had. The result of the wide bed, the recent illness, her own expression which held a haunted introspection.

"Gustav." Her hand closed on his with the old strength. "They've told you?"

"Yes. A chill." He drew in his breath with an audible rasp. "It seems my prayers were answered. Thank God it wasn't—"

125

"Hnaudifida?" Her smile was reassuring. "What are the reports on that?" The outbreaks were under control, no new cases reported for a day now, and the monks, working like men possessed, had organized isolation sheds and manned them with willing volunteers immunized with vaccines obtained from their blood. Details she heard without expression. "I'm glad," she said when he had finished. "We must do something for them."

"The monks? Of course, when you are on your feet, my dear. Some land might be best, a small farm so as to provide food and sustenance. And a little space in the city for them to erect a larger church. We can talk about it later."

She nodded and one hand traced patterns on the smooth cover of the bed. Looking at it she said, "I've been dreaming, Gustav. I think it was a dream. Of Iduna.

He said nothing, waiting.

"She was so lovely. Do you remember when she was a baby how odd she looked? Everyone said how beautiful she was but they were only trying to be kind. But later, when she filled out and could sit upright, there was no need for them to flatter. The child was lovely. So very lovely. Gustav! Oh, Gustav!"

His arms closed around her as her head came to his shoulder and he could feel beneath his hands the wracking as she yielded to grief. Tears which wet the fabric of his blouse and misery which stung his own eyes as he shared the pain he could not alleviate. So many years now. So many, many years.

And again he saw the small shape lying on the floor of his study and the cursed orb of the Tau glowing to one side.

He should have followed her then but he hadn't known, hadn't guessed what happened. A child who had collapsed—first had to come the medical diagnosis, the tests, the investigations. Then he had yielded to Kathryn's dictates and had let others go where he had not. A coward, he thought bitterly. One who had died many times and still held back from dying once.

Now all he could do was to hold his wife and kiss her and wait for the sobbing to quiet and give her what comfort he could until, finally, she slipped into a doze. Chasing the illusion of a lost daughter, perhaps. He had no way of knowing.

But, perhaps, he could give her news when she next woke.

Tamiras was where he had left him, a small figure in the harsh confines of the chamber, flanked by guards who watched as he studied the Tau. From the bank of instruments standing to one side Marita studied dials and called figures at his command.

"No change." Tamiras sucked in his cheeks. "No discernible lift in emitted radiation. No alteration in temperature. No—a complete stasis, my friend. As I could have told you. As I have told you many times in the past. The Tau is a closed system and so, by definition, cannot be affected in any way. If it could it wouldn't be a closed system." His shrug added a single word.

Elementary.

Gustav said tightly, thinking of Kathryn, "This isn't a lecture hall, Tamiras, and you don't have to be clever. As our foremost electronic expert I'd hoped you could help."

"If I could I would—can you doubt that?" Tamiras met his stare, his own eyes direct. "From the beginning I have worked on the problem but, always, the answer is the same. To began investigating the Tau I must risk destroying it. In fact it is possible that only by destroying it can anything be learned."

"No!"

"You refuse as you have done before and I can understand the reasons for your refusal. Can you understand mine for not wanting to waste time on a problem I have no hope of solving? And you could be wrong. Destruction of the Tau could be the only method of achieving the desired end."

"Can you be positive as to that?"

"No. How could I be? The Tau is a mystery which we, as yet, have only tackled with measurements and the application of logic. The measurements prove, if they prove anything, that we are dealing with a closed system. As yet that is the sum total of our knowledge. The rest is speculation. Is Iduna within the Tau? For want of any better explanation as to what happened to her we must assume that she is. Can others follow her? We have idiots and the dead to prove the inadvisability of trying. Can she be rescued? A question without an answer and one based on the viability of the original speculation. If Iduna did not enter the Tau then she cannot be rescued. If she did we do not know how." He ended bleakly,

"There you have it, my friend. The poor fruit of what you are pleased to term an expert mind."

"Logic," said Gustav impatiently. "Pick your premise and by the use of logic you can prove anything you want to. Forget logic—what we need here is intuition. Logic will tell us a thing is impossible but still that thing can be done. Too often logic is nothing but a wall halting progress."

Gently Tamiras shook his head, "No, Gustav, you are wrong?"

"Wrong? What of your own field-baths? I remember when to mention them was to invite scorn and laughter. How could invisible energies relax and comfort? And rafts? They are heavier than air and so obviously could never fly. It is against all logic—so why bother to look for an answer? The men who found it in use of antigrav units didn't listen to that kind of logic and neither will I. We have facts. Work on them. Iduna is in the Tau. How?"

Old ground and Tamiras sighed as he answered the question. But Gustav was strained, too tense for his own good, and the answer might serve to unwind him a little.

"There is only one way. Physically, of course, she remained here so all that could have been transmitted is the mesh of electromagnetic micro-currents housed by her brain. Not all of them, some residue must have remained to activate the autonomic process and we can speculate that the residue must belong to the sub-frame of human development and is in fact a part of the basic metabolic structure. Elg Barham has done some work on the subject and read a paper at the Arteshion University which I was fortunate enough to hear. He contends that the mind, the intelligence, is a later addition to the actual physical body, and therefore could be divorced from it. If true this would explain certain claims made by those who swear they had left their own bodies either to travel vast distances to observe events or to have actually inhabited others and shared their lives and experiences. There could also be an association with the belief that individual awareness does not become erased at death but moves on in some way as a disembodied intelligence. An intelligence which retains, perhaps, the conviction that physically it is still alive which would account for the phenonema we know as "ghosts." The intelligence, trying to communicate, adopts a familiar form or impresses itself on another's sensory apparatus in a recognizable shape."

"A ghost," said Gustav. "You are saying Iduna is a ghost."

"In a manner of speaking she can be nothing else." Tamiras gestured at the Tau. "A mind trapped in a closed environment. A charge in an accumulator, an intermeshed potential—how can I describe it?"

A drop of water in a soaking wet sponge—Gustav could provide his own analogies but none of them helped.

Distance seemed to be important, when she wasn't close it was possible to obtain a degree of detachment and now, lying on the edge of a beach of glittering sand, Dumarest watched the girl as she sported in the surf.

A lovely woman and one who dispensed madness so that when they were close he was helpless to do other than obey her wishes.

Turning he looked at the sky, a bowl of clear azure tufted with fleecy cloud, the sun a glowing ball of lambent yellow fire. The clouds shifted as he concentrated, merging to form a pattern, a construction of lace which shielded the glare of the sun and sent patches of shadow scurrying over the sand. A triumph, but it brought no satisfaction. If anything it demonstrated the magnitude of his power. A few clouds, the wash of the sea, the shape of the dunes—all things of no importance. Yet when he tried to oppose her will Iduna was always the victor.

"Earl!" She came running toward him over the sand. "Earl, come and join me!"

A vision of loveliness, white skin glowing with a rich, soft sheen, dappled with the pearl of water which also graced the dancing tresses of her hair. The uptilted breasts bounded in their pride and her thighs were twin columns of artistic yearning. Naked, unblemished, unashamed. A woman who reached her hands toward him.

"Come, Earl. Let us ride the waves."

A moment and then he was standing on a narrow, pointed board riding the rolling crest as the wave surged to break on the shore. To be back again this time with the girl, her arms locked around his waist as, legs straddled, he maintained his balance on the shifting support. To fall and spout water and laugh and be back again on the long, smooth slope of a breaker.

Pleasure without pain. Joy without effort.

And later, when the heat of her body had consumed him and they lay on a bed of scented heather there was time for talk and words hung like glittering spangles in the sultry summer air.

"This is wonderful!" Iduna stretched, satiated, muscles writhing beneath velvet skin, eyes half-closed in sensual delight. "Earl, you must never leave me. You don't want to leave me, do you? No, of course you don't. You will stay and be my consort and together we shall rule. Rule and have fun."

Live and play games and after? When she had tired of the games?

"Don't you ever miss anyone, Iduna? Your father, for example?"

"Daddy comes to visit me often. We talk and then he goes away but he always comes back when I need him."

"Anyone else? A friend? A—" Dumarest broke off, knowing it was useless. What she wanted she created and if the people were less than real what difference did it make? They were her conception of reality and so far more satisfying than any other. In her universe Gustav would never scold, her friends never be less than attentive, her lovers other than ideal. "Travel, then," he said. "Have you never wanted to travel? To see other worlds and other ways of living?"

"I have traveled."

To Katanga over the Juntinian Sea. To the Burning Mountains and the Eldrach Jungles. To lands of make-believe inhabited by deliciously frightening monsters and patroled by true and loyal guards.

"Really travel, I mean," said Dumarest. "To take a ship and visit another world. One with a different sun and new cultures. To see strange things and beautiful sights. To have adventures."

"I have them." Her hand reached out to touch him. "I have everything I want, Earl."

Even himself in her image. Dumarest saw his body and knew it had changed. The skin was roseate, the scars vanished, the muscle firm and the proportions now arranged in a pattern not designed by a life of arduous activity. His face too now held softness where once harsh reality had set its mark.

"Earl!"

He fought her attraction as he had before, biting on the inner flesh of his cheek, resisting the sweet temptation to yield, to enjoy the moment, to forget everything but the joy of pleasure. For a moment the woman at his side seemed to waver, to become young and gawky and awkward as she lifted herself on the heather, then the moment had passed and Iduna was beautiful again.

"Earl, why be so foolish?" she said quickly. "All this talk of travel—why should you bother? What could you find you haven't here with me? A castle, lands, servants, fine clothing, good food, all the sweets you can eat and think of the wonderful games we can play. Look, you can be King of the Castle if you want and . . ."

He leaned back, letting her words drift over him, using the one great advantage he had over the girl he had come to find. The hard-won experience of years which had hammered an iron resolve into his being. A maturity and determination which Iduna had to lack. A reluctance ever to yield his fate to another.

And he could recognize the trap which had closed around him.

While in Iduna's universe he was helpless to be other than a puppet moving to her whims. To escape her domination he had to establish his own superiority. But how? And even if he did would things be as they seemed?

"Earl, you—" She blinked as he gestured her to be silent. "What is it? Earl?"

"A message," he said. "I am receiving a message."

"From Earth? Earl, I am tired of you playing that silly game. There is no such world."

"There is if I say so,"

"No, there is only if *I* say so." Her face, suddenly, was ugly. "And I say that you will never mention that place again."

"Earth," he said.

"Earl!"

"Earth! Earth! Earth!"

"You're horrible!" Her face wrinkled as her eyes filled with tears. "Everything was so nice and now you've spoiled it all. I hate you!"

"Earth!" he said again. "Earth! Earth! Earth!"

A boy playing a childish game, obtaining a childish revenge by demonstrating his infantile defiance. Dragging her down to his depicted level, keeping her off balance with adult calculation.

"Stop it!" Her voice rose in a raucous scream. "Stop it, I tell you! Stop it at once!'"

"Earth! Earth! Earth!"

The word a bullet fired again and again at her defenses. An irritation which grew until it dominated her being. Dumarest saw her face change, become young, spiteful, twisted with angry passion.

Then it was gone with the sky, the heather, the sea and glittering sand. The sun and breeze and the scent of flowers. All vanished in a flash to be replaced by a writhing mist in which something screamed.

And the thing which screamed was himself.

Dumarest turned, feeling agony sear every nerve, and together with the physical pain came a mental torment which sent him to double and keen and stare as he threshed and spun in the clammy mist. A vapor which burned like acid and held torments unseen but real and things which lived on his body and mind and increased his agony so that he became something less than human in a blind, primitive, mewing, screaming parody of a man.

The dungeon to which all who offended Iduna were sent.

The place he had seen with himself contained in it—the product of a vagrant thought which had anticipated later events or perhaps Iduna had always carried its concept in the back of her mind and his incarceration would be his punishment had he not played her game.

He had been warned and had ignored the warning and now must pay.

But he was free of her domination.

The pain was bad but he could live with agony which did not kill and it would only take a thought to escape. A little concentration and the mist would vanish and the pain and he would be his own master and able to plan and . . . and . . .

The pain! Dear God, the pain!

The screaming went on and he made no effort to stop it.

Made no effort either to halt his weaving and turning in the stinging mist. To have done either would rob his mind of the power to concentrate on a single, overwhelming thought. To escape. To move from this dungeon and Iduna's vengeance and go somewhere else. To escape . . . escape. . . .

And it happened.

The screaming stopped and the mist vanished and he was, suddenly, in limbo. In a region without shape or form but one filled with the aura of lurking horror. A place—no, The Place. Hell.

He had been naughty and Mommy had punished him and locked him in the dark place where things waited to pounce and eat his eyes and drink their moisture and burrow into his body and there lay their eggs which would hatch and turn into maggots which would gnaw at the living flesh and all the time he wouldn't be able to do anything about it. And there would be ghosts which would come and gibber in his ears and suck at his mind so that when they came for him he would be a shambling idiot. And the dark would press close and crush him. And he was blind and would never see again. And there was no sound. And they would forget him and he would die of thirst and starve and have to eat his own hands and be unable to stand even if they did come for him and would grow into horrible shapes and people would laugh and he would be miserable forever and he hated her . . . he hated her . . . he hated her. . . .

The dark place of punishment for a willful child which he had entered. The one filled with the terror of the unknown. A terror he was now sharing and which held all the ghastly fantasies of an imaginative child. Had Iduna ever been locked away in a dark place? Was that why she hated her mother?

Dumarest forced himself to think of Kathryn, to see her face limned before his eyes. A hard face and one which knew little of compassion. The face of a woman who had learned to rule and who would tolerate no weakness in the one she intended should follow her. Spoiled, cossetted, yet Iduna would have felt the weight of the Matriarch's displeasure if she stepped over the line.

And so The Place.

A child's conception of hell—but Dumarest was not a child.

He straightened and rose, feeling solid ground beneath his boots. Overhead the sky began to lighten with a blaze of stars, winking points set in remembered constellations; the Scales, the Archer, the Heavenly Twins. Signs of the zodiac which circled Earth. And the moon. He must not forget the moon.

It glowed in silver luminescence, dark mottlings giving it the appearance of a skull, wisps of brightness haloing it and adding an extra dimension of enchantment. The air which touched his face was soft with summer warmth and carried the odor of growing things. Earth. His world. Earth!

He could create it and be with it and rule it like a god. The hills which rolled endlessly beneath the sky and all covered with woods and forests in which creatures lived and bred. Fields of crops ripening as he watched, rich ears of swollen grain culled from the bounty of the soil. Fruits and seeds and nuts and streams filled with water like wine—all the things of paradise. He could do it. He could make his own world. Why continue the search when there was no need?

"It wouldn't be the same, boy." The captain, sitting on a rock to one side, his head gently shaking in negation. "It just wouldn't be the same."

"It would be as good."

"No. Think about it for a minute and you'll realize why. You thought of fields and forests and streams and warm breezes—was that the Earth you knew? The one you risked death to escape?"

"It could be. It was once."

"Maybe, but you can't be sure of that. Oh, you have clues and they tend to give that impression, but how genuine is it? A world cultivated from pole to pole. Every coast inhabited, every island, every scrap of terrain owned and worked and occupied. Can you even begin to imagine how many people there must have been to achieve that?"

Dumarest glanced at the sky and thought of dawn. The stars paled as the sun warmed the horizon, the moon seeming to gain a transparent unreality as it climbed to cast an orange-ruby-amber sheen over the terrain. In the distance

mountains soared, their summits graced with snow. From a
copse birds began to greet the new day.

"People," said the captain. Despite the sun his face remained in shadow, the features now growing indistinct. "So
many people. How could they ever manage to get along with
each other? Not that it matters. You can't create Earth and
you know it."

"I can!"

"No. You haven't the skill it would take. You haven't the
knowledge and you haven't the time. How long did it take to
make the real Earth? Millions of years—it doesn't matter just
how many. Ages in which each little scrap of living matter
learned to live with other scraps and to become dependent on
them and to achieve a balanced harmony. To create a thing
which cannot be duplicated anywhere. Earth is unique. You
belong to it and you have to find it. Find it, Earl, not construct a replica. Find it . . . find it . . . find it. . . ."

"How?" The figure was becoming as indistinct as the face.
"How?" demanded Dumarest again. "How?"

"You know." The voice was a sigh. "You know."

"Tell me!"

But he had left it too late. The figure slumped as he
touched it to dissolve in a cloud of drifting sparkles which
spun and spread and became a patch of cloud.

Alone Dumarest stared at his world. The cloud had gone
now, dispersed, a thing as insubstantial as the rest. To create
was to waste time playing with toys and yet what else was
there to do? Return to Iduna and again play her games and
follow her rules? To win dominance—but how could he ever
be sure that the girl he ruled was the real person? And how
was he ever to get back? How could he break free of the trap
he was in; the insidiously attractive world of the Tau?"

Chapter Eleven

Nothing!

Kathryn stared bleakly through the transparent partition separating her from Iduna. It was her right to have entered the room and the technicians had assured her there could be no danger of infection, but the risk was one she refused to take. A chill, a fever—to her a temporary indisposition but how could she ever forgive herself if the girl caught the infection? Protected as she was, cosseted, nurtured with the aid of machines, her resistance would be low. It was wiser to keep her distance.

Wiser, but not easy. The child looked so helpless lying on her snow-white bed. So young and so pitifully vulnerable. Kathryn ached to take her in her arms, to run her hand over the rich tresses of her hair, to comfort her, to mother her. An ache made all the more poignant by the dream.

Closing her eyes, she thought about it. A field of dappled flowers, the sun warm in the emerald sky, a soft breeze carrying the perfume of summer. A cloth spread on the sward and all the furnishings of a picnic. And Iduna, running, laughing, playing with a natural, childish grace. A dream so real that she had been reluctant to wake and, waking, had hurried to the room full of hope that Iduna would be sitting up, awake, restored.

Nothing!

Nothing had changed. The slim figure still rested on the soft bed, the eyes closed, the lashes making crescents on the cheeks, the hair a gleaming halo. The dream had been a lie as all dreams were lies. Wishes dragged from the subconscious and given a surrogate life. Illusions which tormented and shattered into the broken mockery of ill-kept promises.

"My lady?" A technician was at her side, face anxious, and

136

Kathryn realized she had been leaning with her forehead resting against the partition. "Are you well?"

"Yes."

"You look pale. A stimulant, perhaps?"

"No! Nothing!" The woman was being kind and Kathryn softened her tone. "I shall be all right in a moment. A little giddiness, that's all."

"To be expected after your recent illness, my lady. The blood sugar is low but that can easily be rectified. A cup of tisane with glucose will adjust the balance. I will order it immediately."

It was easier not to argue and the tisane did help. Kathryn sipped the hot, sweet fluid in an adjoining chamber barely finishing the cup as Gustav arrived. His expression changed to one of relief as he saw her.

"Kathryn! I understand—"

"That I was sick and wandering and delirious," she interrupted. "How rumor exaggerates. I felt a little giddy and sat down to rest with a cup of tisane. You would like some?" She ordered without waiting for his answer. The technician had been right, the glucose had given her strength, and Gustav looked as if he could use a little. Had he, too, been the victim of dreams?

"You left your bed too soon, my dear," he said. "And will try to do too much too quickly. If the Matriarch cannot set an example of intelligent behavior then who can?"

"Don't nag. Gustav. I wanted to see Iduna." She read the question in his face. "I hoped there would be a change," she explained. "It's been so long now since Dumarest went after her and still we wait."

As they had waited for years and it hadn't really been all that long since the man had entered the Tau. Not really long—but, dear God, long enough!

She heard the thin ringing and looked down and realized the cup in her hand was rattling against the saucer. A sure betrayal of the trembling of her hand which in turn was a betrayal of her over-strained nerves. The waiting. Always the waiting and, already, she was sure there could be no hope. Dumarest would follow the others into insanity and death. A condemned slave who had gambled and lost—what did it matter how they treated his body?

Gustav looked at her as she rose. "Kathryn?"

"Something Tamiras mentioned," she said. "Electronic stimulation of muscle and sinew. If we use electroshock therapy on Dumarest the impact might produce an interesting reaction."

"No." Rising, he caught her arm, talking as he followed her from the room. "Kathryn, you can't. The man is at our mercy. To sear his brain with current—no! No, I won't allow it!"

"You won't allow it? *You*?" For a moment her eyes held him and he was reminded that she was the Matriarch and he a lower form of life. "Your wishes have nothing to do with it. My orders will be obeyed. We have waited too long as it is."

"And his brain? You could destroy it with what you intend."

"A chance he must take."

"And our word? Your word as Matriarch?"

"Dumarest is a slave who merited death. He was offered a chance to redeem himself. As yet he has failed to do that. I have beeen patient long enough." Too long and now patience was over. Why didn't Gustav understand? "He is expendable," she reminded. "If he should die what have we to lose?"

He looked odd lying on the bed. An appararent contradiction as a wild creature looked out of place when held in a cage. Standing, watching the technicians as they fussed about their business, Kathryn studied the hard lines of the face, the mouth, the jaw. The face which had looked so bleak and the mouth so cruel when he had held her at his mercy. An animal fighting to survive—could she blame him for that? And could he blame her for having the same attributes as himself? She was a mother fighting for her child and if she had to kill for Iduna's sake then she would not hesitate.

"All ready, my lady." A technician straightened from where she had been applying electrodes to Dumarest's skull. Others snaked from his torso, stomach and groin, a mesh of wire set to monitor his every physical and mental reaction. To one side a machine waited, a battery of pens hovering over an endless roll of paper, and panels studded with dials and telltales added to the laboratory-like appearance of the room. "I suggest we commence with a short burst of high-level current applied directly to the thalamic area."

"Wait!"

"You have another suggestion?" She had denigrated her consort and regretted it. Now Kathryn wished to make amends. "Gustav?"

"Just wait," he begged. "Make more tests on minor physical stimuli. Try hypnotic therapy. Try drugs—but don't rush to burn his brain."

The technician was affronted. She said, stiffly, "We are not ignorant savages and neither are we sadistic torturers. Stimulus applied to the area I have specified has resulted in beneficial results in a great majority of cases of personality maladjustment."

"A great majority," said Gustav. "And the others? Cabbages? Mindless idiots who would be better dead? Can you honestly claim to know exactly what you are doing?" He turned to Kathryn as she made no answer. "At least the woman is honest. She would be more so if she admitted that her treatment was like throwing a jigsaw up into the air. It sometimes could fall into a new and pleasing shape but more often it lands as a jumble."

"You're wasting time, Gustav."

"We have time. A day, a week, a year even, what does it matter? Dumarest is surviving which is more than the others did. By this time they were idiots, already dying, some even already dead. He could have found Iduna and be leading her back to us. Kathryn—dare you risk our daughter for the sake of a little more delay?

A good argument and she pondered it, looking at the wire-wreathed man on the bed. A dedicated servant fighting on her behalf or a self-seeking mercenary only out for what he could get? Neither, she decided, but a man who was doing what had to be done.

"My lady?" The technicians were waiting. Kathryn looked at her hands, the knuckles, the gleam of the polished nails. "Shall we begin?"

"An hour," said Kathryn. "We'll give him an hour."

The defenses were yielding and soon the battle would be over. In the flare of rolling explosions the castle glittered like a solid gem, turrets and spires limned in flame, the triple arch a fading challenge flung against the sky. Shadows clustered over the meadow and in the gloom things raced and rustled and reared with vibrant clickings. Other shapes of nightmare met them, struggles culminating in dissolution, new menaces rising from the ashes of the old. The air quivered with the pulse and throb of war.

A war of fantasy which Dumarest directed from the summit of a mountain, hurling shafts and javelins of destruction against Iduna and her host, sending the figments of his imagination to stalk the terrors created by hers.

It had escalated from small beginnings; troops of armed and armored men riding, charging, falling to rise again. To be stiffened with the sinews of modern destruction which he knew all too well; the mercenary bands in which he had served providing the template for new armies more savage and vicious than those born from romantic imagery. Then they, in turn, yielded to images of delirium; horrors such as he had first experienced in the Tau, the product of buried fears and whispered fantasies; men with triple heads and spined hides, birds like lizards, dragons spouting fire, spiders which dropped from the clouds and stung like scorpions.

War which waged with unremitting fury and turned the area into a cratered and fuming waste in which the castle alone stood untouched and shining with an inner, lambent glow.

Dumarest hurtled toward it at a thought.

"Iduna! Will you yield?"

Serpents lanced toward him where he stood facing the arched doorway now blocked by the upraised drawbridge. They darted from the battlements, writhing streamers of flame which seared and hissed and fell to the foot of the hemisphere of protection he maintained about his person. From the soil darted things with many legs which scrabbled and reared to fall in puffs of ash and his guardians blasted them.

Things of the mind—when all else had been tried what more terrible than the creatures of childish terrors?

"Iduna! Yield!"

"No!" She stood on the highest battlement and her hair was a pennon of midnight glory. "Earl, I won't let you win!"

A game—always to her everything was a game and she was right. What else could life be but a game with death as the inevitable winner? A gamble to see how long it could be extended and how much accomplished in the time so won.

But Dumarest had had enough of childish games.

To win. To beat her to her knees. To make her surrender

her will and then to discover how to lead them both from the Tau. One way to escape, perhaps, the other he preferred not to think about.

"Iduna!"

She was stubbornly defiant. Soldiers sprang like weeds from the ground to be mown down and left in winnowed heaps and piles of bizarre armor and shapes and weapons. Dumarest fired a torpedo at the triple arch and saw the sky explode in searing, blue-white flame which died to leave the arch untouched, the air filled with drifting motes of burning destruction.

"Iduna?"

"This is silly, Earl." Again she appeared to lean over the glistening stone. "We haven't any rules and neither of us can beat the other. Of course I could—"

And he was deep underground with fires glowing at his feet and only the bubble of protection allowing him to breathe. Then he was back on the surface.

"—But it's no good. Why did you leave me, Earl?"

"I didn't like where you put me."

"It was only for a little while. You'd upset me and I was angry but I'm not angry now. Come and have some tisane."

Come into my parlor . . .

"Earl?"

"Why not? Lower the drawbridge and I'll come inside and we can talk. I've thought of something really nice we can do."

"Something new?" The woman stood upright as the child within her clapped her hands. "That's lovely! Hurry, Earl! Hurry!"

The skies quieted as he crossed the lowered drawbridge, the sound and fury of war muttering into a calm tranquility as he mounted the stairs to where Iduna waited on the battlements. Shamarre was attending her, the beast at her side and others thronged close; men with bandaged wounds, women with haggard faces. Warriors and their ladies who changed even as he watched into bland courtiers and simpering maidens.

"The game, Earl! Tell me about the new game!"

Iduna was dressed as a warrior queen, retaining the scaled armor which molded itself to her body, the cloak of shimmering silk adorned with abstract devices. Her head was bare and her hair flowed in rippling tresses. Watching her, Dumarest concentrated on seeing the child, catching glimpses of a long-legged girl dressed up in her mother's clothing. Flashes which dimmed against the immediate impression of firm flesh and rounded limbs—the child as she imagined herself to be. The woman she had become.

"The game?"

Dumarest said, "We fight on neutral ground. The winner is obeyed."

"Fight? Really fight?" A hand lifted to place a thumb within the carmined mouth. "Like men fight with women before they make love? Will we make love again, Earl? Like we did before?"

"The game, Iduna."

"I like it. A personal challenge. Yes, I like it. But we should balance the odds because it wouldn't be fair for me to face you. I'm too small and too light and far too weak. And the wager? What shall we decide."

"The winner to be obeyed."

"I know. You said that. But obeyed in what? In all things, Earl? In all things?"

"Yes."

"And I may use a champion?" Her laughter rose as he nodded. "Very well then, Earl. He is behind you. Begin!"

Dumarest spun—and looked at himself.

Facing him was a man who wore gray, who stooped to lift the knife from his boot, who attacked with sudden, blinding speed, the blade whining as it ripped through the air, the tip slicing a long gash in the breast of his tunic.

Dumarest sprang back, his own blade lifting, steel clashing as the weapons met, to part, to reflect a glitter of light as they joined again with the sound of chiming cymbals.

A moment in which muscle strained against muscle and face looked at face eye to eye. A hard face and hard eyes and a mouth savagely cruel in its determination to kill. His face and yet not exactly so. There were minor differences: the finer arch to brows, the lines less deeply scored, the nostrils less flared. Small touches which added to a gentler type of masculine attractiveness as judged by a certain kind of woman. One unaccustomed to the harsh realities of an unprotected existence.

Not himself then but a copy and Dumarest could guess why. A replacement to fill the gap he had made by leaving the castle. A doll modeled on her need to be always kind, always obedient, always the attentive lover and now the protective champion.

A facsimile which would kill if he gave it the chance.

The blades parted as Dumarest swung wide his own, backing as he did so and feeling the bulk of the parapet pressing against him as the stone halted his progress. A barrier along which he slid as again the other attacked, dodging to attack in turn, seeing his blade touch a cheek and create a rill of blood.

"First blood, Iduna! I've won!"

"We didn't decide that, Earl. You fight until one yields."

And the surrogate would never yield.

He attacked again, the face cold, hard, intent on plunging the knife home in soft and yielding flesh. A glitter and the point raked up over the stomach, the edge grating on protective mesh. Dumarest flung back his head as the blade lifted toward his face, saw the glint of steel and struck back at the body before him. A cut which opened plastic and revealed the same mesh he wore himself.

"You're equally matched, Earl!" Iduna, watching, smiled her delight. "But you can't both win."

And, if he lost?

Dumarest dismissed the thought as he faced his opponent. Even to think of losing was to give the other an advantage, for a man dwelling on the possibility of defeat robs himself of that much concentration on victory. And he ignored the likeness to himself. He was not fighting a brother and he was not fighting himself. He was only fighting a man who looked as he did and one who did not fight as well.

Iduna had done her best but it was not good enough.

Dumarest turned, pivoting on a heel, feeling air brush his cheek as, again, the man aimed at his face. A stupidity, the target was too small and contained too much bone and a cut could do little harm unless it hit the eyes. As the blade threw light into his eyes he slashed upward, drawing back the blade as it hit, the edge catching the wrist and biting deep into the naked flesh. Maimed, the man dropped the knife and backed, his face now taut with fear.

"Shamarre!"

Dumarest heard the cry as he stepped in for the kill seeing the beast at the woman's side launch itself toward him. A creature twice the weight of a man with sharp claws on all four paws and fangs which could crush bone and sever a limb. Dropping, he rolled, felt the jar as the animal landed, slashed out as it struck at his face.

Blood dripped from the wounded paw and the beast snarled, foul breath gusting from gaping jaws, the lash of the tail a club which pounded Dumarest's arm. A blow followed by another as a boot slammed into his ribs. A boot which lifted to grind a heel into his face.

Dumarest dropped the knife as it descended, catching the foot in both hands, twisting as he rose to send his opponent hurtling over the battlements to fall screaming to the moat below. The beast sprang before he could recover the knife, claws ripping at arm and side, the impact knocking him over to sprawl flat on his back. As the animal sprang again Dumarest lifted both legs, feet close together, knees bent, kicking out with the full force of back and thighs as the creature came within range. Blood dappled the muzzle and before the half-stunned creature could recover Dumarest was on his feet, knife in hand and body tense.

"Iduna—"

"Keep fighting, Earl. My champion wasn't specified."

A cheat—but why was he surprised? He could never win and even if he did she would not agree to the bargain. A hope lost and a new danger to face.

Air blasted as wings drummed and this time when the creature sprang it hovered, striking, filling the air with razor claws and stabbing fangs, claws which ripped at head and face and shoulders as the fangs snapped at arm and side, sinking in, lifting even as Dumarest plunged home the knife, twisting it so as to release a fountain of blood from the laboring heart.

But, dying, the creature held on.

Dumarest lifted his legs and kicked as the edge of the battlements came close. He felt them brush past beneath him as the winged creature bore him from the castle. To carry him far to one side where rocks studded the ground like a nest of broken teeth.

To drop him where they waited.

"His eyes!" Gustav's voice was sharp. "Look at his eyes!"

They were moving beneath the closed lids in the rapid eye movements which told of dreams. A technician stared then turned to check a bank of dials. Another engaged the waiting machine and the banked pens began tracing their patterns on the rolling paper.

"Well?" Kathryn was impatient. "What does all this mean?"

"He's waking up!" Gustav fought to control his voice. "Don't you see? Dumarest is waking up!"

He was triumphant but he had reason for his emotion. It had been a long, tense hour with the technicians urging Kathryn to let them begin and she wavering between her decision and natural impatience. Twice he'd had to remind her of the value of a Matriarch's word, each time busying himself with make-work, acting with assumed confidence as he'd played with the waiting instruments, giving her a reason for delay until a new "setting" had been tested. A pretense the technicians had noticed but had thought better to ignore.

"Waking?" Kathryn glanced at a technician. "Is that so?"

"There is no evidence to support the contention." The woman was thin-faced and with a manner radiating hostility to all who dared to question her professional capability. "True, there are signs of REM but—" She saw Kathryn's expression and hastily explained. "REM, my lady, rapid eye movements, are a sure sign of a dreaming person. However it does not follow that a dreaming person is one about to wake."

Gustav said acidly, "Did the others display similar symptoms?"

"I'm not sure. I could check. My own work lay in calibrating blood-sugar levels."

"Don't bother to check," said Gustav. "I can tell you the answer. No REM were noted in any other volunteer. When and if they woke it was without that preliminary symptom. Kathryn! Don't you understand what this could mean?"

Success!

It could be all summed up in that one word. A man had entered the Tau and was returning and—she hardly dared to hope, Iduna could be returning with him. But why didn't he waken? What was keeping him so long?

Gustav caught her arm as she extended it to touch Dumarest's cheek.

"No."

"Why not?"

"There is a better way." His own arm reached to rest, the palm over the lips, the thumb and forefinger nipped to close the nostrils. "A trick a mercenary taught me years ago. It wakes a man up and keeps him silent as it does so. There You see?"

Dumarest had opened his eyes.

For a long moment Kathryn stared into them, wondering if again she would see the horrible vacuity she had seen so often before. The telltale sign of an empty brain. Of an idiot returned to once again blast her hopes.

"Earl!" Gustav was at her side, his tone urgent. "Come back, Earl! Come back!"

Back from a dream in which he had tumbled through air to crash on waiting rocks. But it had been no dream and the rocks and the impact had been real. As real as any rocks could ever be—and the death had been as genuine.

"Earl?" Gustav was staring at him, the Matriarch at his side. She looked paler than Dumarest remembered, older, her eyes containing a bruised hurt. She said quickly before Gustav could speak again, "Did you see her? Iduna, did you meet?"

He saw the smile irradiate her face as he nodded.

"And?"

"She sends you her regards, my lady." Then, adding to the lie, "Her regards and her fondest love and affection for you both."

Chapter Twelve

"You met," said Kathryn. "You actually saw her and talked to her and played with her?" Her voice held an aching envy. "Tamiras, you hear that?"

"I hear it." The man selected a fruit from the bowl before him and carefully removed the rind. "I hear it but that isn't to say I believe it.

"Tamiras!"

"I am a scientist and, as such, tend to be skeptical. If that is a fault then I am guilty." Juice ran from the sections he parted with deft fingers. Lifting one to his mouth he added, "And Dumarest has reason to please you."

"And reason to lie?"

She glanced at Dumarest where he sat at the table. He, the scientist, Gustav and herself were alone. The meal had been a good one, meats and wines and fine breads to put energy into his body and flesh on his bones. A celebration, Gustav had called it, a time for them to learn all he had discovered. But if Dumarest had lied . . . ?

He saw the tension of her hand where it rested beside her plate, the reflected light flash from gems as her fingers closed in an unconscious betrayal of her doubt and anger.

To Tamiras he said, flatly, "Are you calling me a liar?"

"A liar?" The man shrugged and ate another segment of fruit. "No, my friend, I do not, but false impressions can often seem real. Let us review the situation. You were forced to enter the Tau. Subconsciously you feared the penalty of failure because in all sentient life forms the need to survive is paramount. So you carried out your mission with complete success. Or you are convinced you did—you appreciate the difference?"

That and more. Dumarest glanced at the hand lying beside the plate, thin, blotched, but it held his life. If the Matriach

147

doubted his sincerity a word would send him to execution. But how to erase the doubts Tamiras had sown?

He said, "I saw Iduna lying on her bed and that is all. You agree?"

"I don't understand what point you are trying to make."

"Is it so hard? I never saw her as a child. I wasn't even on this world. My only contact with her was when I was taken to see her."

"So?"

"So let us talk of her childhood. She had friends; a bear, a toad, a doll fashioned in the likeness of a clown. She had a room with papered walls and the paper bore a design of fish and shells. She held parties for her friends and used a service adorned with small flowers with blue petals and scarlet leaves." He heard the sharp inhalation of indrawn breath from where Kathryn sat. Without looking at her he added, "And she was fond of small, iced cakes."

"What child isn't?" Tamiras shrugged. "What you say proves nothing."

"All of it? The dolls? The room?"

"You could have picked that up from gossip. The guards—"

"Have never seen Iduna's old room." Kathryn was sharp in her interruption. Looking at Dumarest she said, "How do you know?"

"I saw it." Dumarest gestured at the table, the articles on its polished surface. "The room, the paper, the service, the dolls—all were as real as the things before us."

"And Iduna? You saw her? You *saw* her!"

"Yes, my lady."

"But could not pursuade her to return," said Tamiras dryly. "May I dare to ask why you failed?"

"She didn't want to."

"Didn't want to return? To her home? Her loving parents?"

"No."

"And you couldn't make her? A child?"

"A god!" Dumarest glanced at Gustav, spoke to the Matriarch. "That is what Iduna is now—the supreme ruler of her universe. A goddess, if you want to be precise, and who can force a goddess to do anything against her will? What she wants—is. Can you even begin to understand what that means? To have the world in which you live exactly to your liking. To have it populated by those who care for you. Who exist only because of you. To want for nothing. To have no fear. To have no pain, no tears, no sadness. To be free of regret. To be innocent of guilt."

"Heaven," whispered Gustav. "A place in which all that is supposed to be. Could she have found it?"

Kathryn was more direct. "Is she happy?"

"Yes, my lady."

"A child, alone—"

"With everything to live for," emphasized Dumarest. "With all the toys she could ever want. All the companions she could ever need. A girl as happy as anyone could ever be." He saw the glint of reflected light as the curved fingers relaxed and knew the immediate danger was past. "She is content, my lady—that I swear. There is no need for you to torment yourself with imagined terrors. No need for further tears."

But they were there just the same, dimming her eyes, pearls of relief which dampened her cheeks.

Gustav, watching, poured and passed fresh goblets of wine. An act designed to attract attention to himself, the new subject he broached; one of lesser emotional content. To Dumarest he said, "Tamiras has explained how the Tau must hold the mental energy-pattern of the ego but why did the others die or go insane?"

"Fear."

"Just that?"

"It was enough." Dumarest stared into his goblet and saw dim shapes reflected in the ruby surface. "We all contain the terrors we fear the most. The others entered the Tau expecting danger and found it. They anticipated horror and it waited for them; things of nightmare created by their own minds, spawned by their own imaginations. The battles they fought were with themselves and were impossible to win. So they were defeated. Their minds," he explained. "They lost their minds. Their egos, trapped in the Tau, lost all sense of direction or purpose."

"But not Iduna." Tamiras helped himself to another fruit. Like the juice it contained his tone held acid. "She, naturally, was immune."

"She was young."

"And?"

"Young," repeated Dumarest. "A child accustomed to illusion and make-believe. One to whom fantasy was a normal part of life as it is with every child. She could accept what drove others insane."

"As you could?" Juice dribbled from his fingers and Tamiras dabbled them in a bowl of scented water before drying them on a napkin. "I find it hard to accept you as a child."

"I became one. I thought as one and felt as one and so entered the Tau."

And became a god with his own universe and his own incredible power.

Candles had been set for decoration and Dumarest stared into a dancing flame seeing in the lambent glow the woman he had left, the love she had given him, the spite she had displayed. Had he really existed in her world or had she occupied his? Had the game of war sprung from his mind or hers? Was she even now ruling from her throne in her castle with the facsimile of himself she had created at her side? Had she ever really accepted him as being more than a figment of her imagination?

"Earl?" Gustav was looking at him from where he sat and Dumarest glanced away from the dancing flame. "The Tau," said Gustav when sure he had gained attention. "What is it, Earl? Did you discover that?"

"For certain, no, but I think it must be a toy."

"What?"

"A toy—and a trap." Dumarest looked at Tamiras. "One used by a so-called friend to gain revenge. An expert in his field who knew exactly what he was doing."

"A trap?" Tamiras shook his head, outwardly calm, indifferent, as again he dipped his fingers into the scented water. "You talk like a fool. The thing is alien, that is obvious, but a trap? For whom?"

"For a child," said Dumarest, flatly. "The daughter of the woman you hate."

"Hate?" Tamiras's eyes darted to the woman, back to Dumarest. "Are you insane?"

"Earl—"

Gustav fell silent at Kathryn's gesture. "Iduna," she said.

"You're talking about Iduna. My daughter. My child. Tamiras—"

"The man lies! He is deranged. Crazed by his experiences. A man who claims to have talked with a ghost can hardly be given credence." He rose with an abrupt gesture, water streaming from his hands. "I refuse to listen to this nonsense! If I may be excused?"

"Remain in your place!" She looked at Dumarest as Tamiras, reluctantly, obeyed. As he settled in his chair she said, "Earl, he could be right when he says your brains have been addled but you have said too much not to say more. Explain!"

Cutlery rested on the table: sharp-edged steel used for cutting meat, fruit, vegetables; forks, thin knives, spoons with reflective bowls. Dumarest glanced at them, noting their position, the placement of hands, moving his own as he took nuts and held them one against the other in his palm.

"The background," he said. "Gustav is known as a collector of old things so what more simple than to bribe a captain to take him the Tau with an elaborate story of how it was found? But who would hold such a thing in secret for any length of time? Someone not resident on Esslin, perhaps, but who came to live here later. He would have studied it, learned something of its workings. Then, with it safely delivered, a word in a receptive ear and the rest was inevitable. Who was close enough to Iduna to have given her that word?"

Tamiras said, harshly, "This is ridiculous! Accusations without proof!"

"Have I accused you?"

"Who else?" Tamiras appealed to the Matriarch. "Can't you see what he's doing? The man has lied and needs to create a diversion. By accusing me he hopes to gain your trust. But where is his proof?"

"Earl?"

Dumarest looked at the hard face, the hard eyes. The face and eyes of a woman who had sent men to be impaled, who would watch him die if he failed to convince her.

"Proof?" He didn't look at the scientist who sat glowering at him. "Iduna supplied that. She told me how friendly Tamiras was with her. How he used to bring her toys and small surprises. And think of the time it happened. It was late, remember? The sun was setting and the study would have been filled with gloom. It was summer and the days long so it would have been late. Iduna, a child, would not have been permitted too much liberty. It must have been close to her normal bedtime. Why should she have broken routine to run into the study? What better motive than to see the new toy? Who told her it would be there? Who explained how to hold it so as to feel the exciting tingle against the skin? How to look into it so as to see all the pretty pictures?"

"Tamiras?" Gustav glanced at the man, frowning. "But why, Earl? Why?"

"Iduna didn't know that."

Kathryn could guess. The mother who had rebelled, her banishment and later death, the return of her son to a world which offered neither land nor status. God, why had she been so blind!

Gustav was slow to understand. "But Iduna? Why would he want to hurt a child?"

The nuts crushed in Dumarest's hand. "Think of the years of hell you and your wife have lived through and you have your answer."

Revenge, what else, and he could have sown the seeds of hnaudifida to compound his hatred. A realization Tamiras saw mirrored on her face and he rose as she shouted, one hand diving beneath his blouse.

"Guards! Shamarre!"

She came as he jerked free the weapon, too late to prevent or protect her mistress from the killing beam of the laser, seeing a sudden glitter of steel, the blood, hearing his curse as the weapon fell from his limp hand. The meat knife Dumarest had snatched up and thrown had penetrated the wrist and severed the tendons.

Tamiras looked at the wound, at the man who had given it. "Why?" he demanded. "In God's name, why? What are these people to you?"

"Nothing." Dumarest was blunt, his face hard as he remembered what he had seen in the Tau, the horrors which had ruined adult minds. "But you sent a child into hell!"

Soon it would change; walls of carved and fretted stone forming an area which enclosed a shrine, a place made holy by what it contained but, as yet, the place had not changed.

The Tau still rested on its support bathed in a cone of brilliance, catching it, reflecting it in darting rainbow shimmers. A jewel of enigmatic beauty; the instruments to measure and calibrate, to test and monitor set like sentinels all around. Looking at it Kathryn thought of a snake subtle and deadly in its beauty, a snare, a contradiction.

"A toy," she mused. "You were joking, of course."

"No." Dumarest had accompanied her at her command and now stood at her side. Shamarre, the Matriarch's shadow, was alert, remembering an earlier occasion when he had made a mockery of her protective role. "An alien toy," he said. "But a toy just the same."

"One which kills?"

"A game can kill. And the Tau did not actually kill those volunteers; they fell victim to their own fears." He had explained it too often and was tired of it. Why was the obvious so difficult for certain types of mind to grasp? "Think of it as a book," he urged. "You pick up a book and are enveloped in an author's world. You taste the flavors he mentions, see the images he portrays, meet the people he has created, experience the situations he provides. Reading, you use your imagination to clothe the skeletons and to fill the gaps; the form of a castle seen at sunset, the hues staining the sky, the garb worn by the host of inhabitants he does not bother to mention but which must exist. A thousand small details."

"The servant who opens the door," she said. "The workers who maintain the city. The pedestrians. The poor. Those who die from accident or disease. I understand."

"And think of a chess board on which players fight symbolical wars. Or a construction kit with which children can build palaces."

Analogies, but that of a book was the best. Something to pick up and delve into during odd moments. Something to provide an escape from boredom or reality grown too harsh. Worlds of excitement waiting to be explored. She had read much as a child. What was it an instructor had once told her? Books are the refuge of the lonely.

Was Iduna lost in a book?

If so she could be roused and Dumarest had learned how to reach her. She could go with him and find her child and together they could plan a new life. If Dumarest agreed— there was no need of that. What she ordered would be done!

"No." His voice was soft, a whisper in the echoing stillness. "I won't do it."

"Do what? Have you read my mind?"

"Your face mirrored your thoughts—and why else am I here? But I won't take you into the Tau."

"We made a bargain," she reminded. "You to rescue Iduna in return for certain rewards. You have yet to rescue her."

"I did my best."

"And if I think it not good enough?"

"You can go to hell!" His sudden viciousness startled her and she glanced around to see Shamarre standing close, the glint of a weapon in her hand. Once had been enough; she would not be caught wanting again. Dumarest followed the Matriarch's eyes and guessed her thoughts. "Try it," he invited. "Order me back into a collar and see what happens."

"You'd kill me?"

"I'd try."

And probably succeed before dying in turn. She remembered the speed with which he had acted when Tamiras had been unmasked. The thrown knife had been a blur, hitting even before she'd noticed he'd moved his hand. A flicker which had robbed an enemy of the power to hurt. What greater harm could he have done had Dumarest chosen to remain silent?

Quietly she said, "Earl, I owe you too much for us to quarrel, all I can do is to appeal. Iduna is my child and I yearn to see her, surely you can understand that? It's a natural, mother's need. If—"

"She is happy as she is. Leave her alone."

"And me?"

"You have your memories. The knowledge that your daughter is safe and happy as I've told you. Take care of her body and you'll do all that can be done."

He was telling her something, warning her, perhaps, and she said with sudden insight, "She hates me, is that it?" She saw by his tension she had scored. "Don't be so astonished— all children hate their parents at times as I've cause to know and, as a mother, I was far from being the best. Iduna was willful and headstrong and impatient to rule. Always she wanted that. To give orders without first learning how to obey. An essential—how else to avoid an absolute lack of restraint?"

A barrier which no longer existed. And how could a child have understood the necessity of such teaching? To realize that untrammeled despotism led inevitably to cabals, assassinations, civil wars.

Kathryn said, "I will treble your reward if you take me into the Tau." She read the answer in his face and was suddenly aware of the reason behind the refusal. Not the simple fear she had imagined or the willful stubbornness of ignorance but something far beyond that; the awful longing once again to act the god. How had he managed to tear himself from such temptation?

"I died," he said when she asked. "I chose to die. I think it is the only way a human can leave the Tau."

Died? She restrained the obvious question. The mechanics were unimportant but how had it felt? To have willingly faced extinction. To have actually experienced it—but had it been like that? Had he really died or had he been convinced, deep inside, that it was just an extension of the game? But if the world of the Tau were as real as the one she now experienced wouldn't death hold the same terror?

Dumarest said, "My lady, you spoke of a reward."

"What?" She was startled at the intrusion into her thoughts, the abrupt change of subject. "Reward—you are impatient to leave?"

"Yes, my lady." Before her gratitude waned in the face of her urgent desires. "There is nothing more I can do here."

He had earned the reward and Gustav would condemn her for withholding it. He had the money together with Dumarest's clothing, his knife, a certificate of citizen status and a grant of land which would be his should he choose to stay. Bribes which she now recognized as worthless. He would not stay. If the Tau couldn't hold him then nothing could and to use restraint was to invite destruction. Yet she was reluctant to see him go.

"Earl—we shall remember you."

"For a while, my lady, perhaps. But you have other things to occupy your attention."

The ravages the disease had left, the organization waiting to be done, the arranging of affairs so as to ensure the safety of her rule. Tamiras had been one but there would be others and they would have to be discovered and dealt with. Duties—always there were duties. But, for now, she would indulge herself in a brief time of pleasure. As a moth turning toward a flame she turned to face the Tau.

"My lady?"

"You are so impatient, Earl. So impetuous. Shamarre, our guest is leaving us. Escort him to where Gustav waits in the study."

"My lady! And leave you alone?"

At another time the protest would have annoyed her and brought a swift rebuke. Now she only smiled. "Alone? How can I be alone? I have Iduna with me. My child."

Trapped to wander in the maze of her mind, but Dumarest said nothing of that. He turned as he reached the end of the chamber to look back at where the Matriarch stood like some priestess at the ancient altar of a pagan god. The light caught her, haloed her with a rainbow nimbus, bound her as if entranced and, already, she was doomed.

An hour, a day, a week—the period was unimportant but, inevitably, she would succumb. She would approach the Tau and caress it and become as a child and enter into the world it provided. A victim. A god. Always a slave.

"Hurry!" Shamarre was impatient to return. "Gustav will be waiting."

As were the ships, the stars, his freedom.

DAW PRESENTS MARION ZIMMER BRADLEY

"A writer of absolute competency . . ."—Theodore Sturgeon

Recommended for Star Warriors!

The Novels of Gordon R. Dickson

The Commodore Grimes Novels of A. Bertram Chandler

The Dumarest of Terra Novels of E. C. Tubb

The Daedalus Novels of Brian M. Stableford

If you wish to order these titles,

please use the coupon in

the back of this book.

Attention:

DAW COLLECTORS

Many readers of DAW Books have written requesting information on early titles and book numbers to assist in the collection of DAW editions since the first of our titles appeared in April 1972.

We have prepared a several-pages-long list of all DAW titles, giving their sequence numbers, original and current order numbers, and ISBN numbers. And of course the authors and book titles, as well as reissues.

If you think that this list will be of help, you may have a copy by writing to the address below and enclosing fifty cents in stamps or coins to cover the handling and postage costs.

DAW BOOKS, INC.   Dept. C
1633 Broadway
New York, N.Y. 10019

Presenting JOHN NORMAN in DAW editions . . .